I0629774

Ros Barker's

The Mind's Eye

Also By **Ros Barker**

The God Complex: Family Secrets

This Book is dedicated to my mother Tam Barker.

I love you Mother...Wish you were still here!

Chapter One

I'm not a handsome man, thought Detective
Bordeaux. He'd been a detective so long now he
answered to Detective more often than his first name.
I wonder if anyone even remembers my name.

Women often told him he looked like Harrison Ford.
He, like Ford, had once been a carpenter before
getting into his present line of work and like Ford,
had a few scars. Harrison Ford carried his scars
visibly on his face, Bordeaux's scars were unseen. He
carried the invisible scars written hard on his heart
and burned into his brain. The scars came from seeing
the absolute worst things humanity could do to one
another. Years of putting a dab of Vicks vapor rub
under his nose before he walked into a crime scene,
not knowing what he was going to encounter had
jaded the old man. Detective Bordeaux had seen
every bad thing a human being could do to another,
and he managed to hide this knowledge from all but
the most pious observer. *If the world could see my
scars they wouldn't even speak to me,* he thought.

Bordeaux had *something* most women found
attractive. Old, young, rich, poor, tall, short, skinny,
fat, White, Black, Hispanic—it didn't matter—they
all found him charming. Was it the shy smile, or his
uncanny ability to make everyone around feel at ease?
It definitely wasn't his athletic build. He wasn't *out of
shape*, but he definitely wasn't *in shape*. He had the
typical body of a man closer to retirement than he'd

like to admit. Bordeaux on occasion decided to watch what he ate and exercise, but always within a few weeks discovered the sacrifices aren't worth missing out on crisp bacon, and pancakes smothered in warm sorghum molasses.

He looked up into the rear view mirror of his state issued Chevrolet Tahoe and winked at his reflection. His gray eyes twinkled as he thought about how Sue, the waitress at *Fifes,* had brushed up against him as she leaned over to place his short stack of pancakes with bacon in front of him. She'd been flirting with him for years, and he knew he'd eventually break her heart. A man didn't have to be a detective to read Sue's body language and deduce she wanted more than the $2 tip he left on the red table cloth each morning.

Last month she'd asked him if he would take her home after her shift ended at 3:00 P.M. because her car was in the shop and she really didn't feel comfortable riding the bus. Bordeaux knew where a ride home would go. In an effort to let her down easy, he explained he wouldn't be back in time. In North Alabama someone was murdering young girls. He'd still be up there when she got off work. Disappointment was obvious in her deep blue eyes.

Probably the main thing women liked about Detective Bordeaux was the passion for his work. He had created a name for himself. As an investigator, he had not even one unsolved case. Nevertheless, Sue's request made him uncomfortable, so for ten days he made a conscious effort to find other restaurants in which to indulge his morning cravings for pancakes and bacon, but breakfast at the *Waffle House* wasn't the same, and they didn't have molasses. He'd been eating at *Fife's* for more than a decade now, they knew him here and brought his breakfast without the hassle of ordering. So today he had come back home.

Sue smiled when she saw him crinkling up her sky blue eyes and perfectly shaped nose as she flashed her deep dimples. She hugged him tight. "Have a seat sugar," she said, "I'll get your order in." For a moment he wondered if he could ever feel anything for the nice lady who brought him his breakfast every morning.

Even though it was a busy morning Sue sat down across from him when she set his breakfast on the table. "I missed you sugar," she said. Sue didn't give him a chance to reply before she said, "Bordeaux, why don't you meet me for a drink at *The Blue Monkey* tonight. You've been coming in here for years always sitting in my section. I ain't gettin' any younger honey. You been too long without a wife, and I been too long without a man. If I ain't good enough for you, well I guess you need to go on back to the Waffle House."

Bordeaux was surprised, and he wasn't a man easily surprised. He had really believed not coming into the restaurant for ten days would get the message across

to her. "You know," he said, "I believe I will."
Tonight he would be going on a date with a lady who
had pursued him for more than a year. He wasn't sure
yet how he felt about meeting her, but then it had
been more than two years since his wife had
passed…maybe it was time. Sue was lot like his wife
had been, she worked too hard for too little and cared
too much

Why, am I still not remarried? Sue is sweet and well-built with an obvious adoration for me. She'll make me a good wife, it isn't like I don't know her…it would be nice to have someone at home again, someone warm in the bed when I come home after one of those long nights standing in the drizzling rain trying to make some sense out of a corpse in a ditch alongside I-59…make my empty house a home again. Ahhh…enough of the what-if game old boy…get your mind on the little girls… Bordeaux was brought back
to the present as he heard his cell phone ring its
musical rendition of the University of Alabama's
fight song.

"Hello."

"Saw your picture in the paper."

"Who is this?"

"I am Azrael," said the crystal-clear voice, "and I
know where the sweet little Jarnigan girl is."

"You know I'm coming for you?"

10

"It doesn't matter, there's nothing you can do to stop me Detective Bordeaux, and someday you won't have to come for me, I'll find you."

"Come on, I'm not a defenseless little girl."

Chapter Two

Alabama Bureau of Investigation

Birmingham, Alabama

"*He's so tall and handsome as hell, he's so bad and he does it so well.*" Bordeaux sang as he maneuvered his Tahoe into the parking lot and parked close to the building by patrol cars from Winston County and Marion County Sheriff's Department. His singing unnerved the other policemen sometimes. Bordeaux wasn't musically gifted, and he was completely tone-deaf, but music helped him think and today's song was a new song from Taylor Swift.

"What have we got, Ben?" asked Bordeaux as he walked into his office.

"We've got, well, we've got nothing we didn't have yesterday."

All we have is what we already know and a new dead girl. No new evidence. No witnesses. No…No…Nothing! Right now we've got twenty-five dead girls and nothing except twenty-five extremely angry families and nothing. I mean…what else can I say? We have physical evidence, we have DNA evidence, and nothing which helps us find a killer…I mean I don't know what else to tell you."

Bordeaux closed his eyes and sang, "*I can see the end as it begins, my one condition is...*I swear I never met Taylor before, but I know she's singing about me."

"God Bordeaux, enough with the Taylor Swift...Can't we have a no Taylor Tuesday?"

"No, it's Friday...Oh wow, look out here she comes Ben."

Ben turned to see a brunette in her early twenties come swaying down the hallway. Rita wore a black racer long sleeved crop top with her flat stomach and belly-button ring prominently on display above a skin-tight pencil skirt. As she strode into the office Ben tried to move out of her way, but she was having none of that.

"Captain wants to see the two of you," Rita said as she pushed her body against Ben, making sure she was aware of her interest in him. "He said pronto, Tonto!"

"Jesus Rita, can you possibly be any more racially denigrating?"

"What are you talking about? You're not an Indian," laughed Bordeaux.

"Thanks for the information, Bordeaux...Okay Rita we'll be down there in a few minutes."

"No problemo señor," Rita said. "You know if you don't ask me out pretty soon I'm going there's something wrong with me Detective McElroy."

"Jeez Rita…you're a lovely girl…a beautiful girl…you're just not my type."

"Honey I'm every man's type."

"No…you're not."

"What's wrong with me…you just said I was beautiful…maybe if you'd give me a chance?"

"Nothing is *Wrong* with you Rita…you're just not my type."

"Exactly what is your type?"

"My type is really none of your business…besides I don't date co-workers…it's not professional."

"Ben…I promise there won't even be a whiff of sexual harassment…I'm coming on to you…I'm not filing any lawsuits, I'm looking for a good guy. I think you're the man I'm looking for."

"Rita…the bureau has a policy forbidding co-workers dating."

"Bureau smureau…I don't have the greatest job here. Why not just one date…Bordeaux isn't going to tell are you?" she turned and looked at the older detective.

"I promise I won't say a word," Bordeaux said with a grin on his face thinking about Sue.

Ben pushed past Rita and out into the hallway, "Come on Bordeaux, she said the captain wants to see us," he said as he stalked down the hallway.

"Bordeaux," she questioned, "I know I'm coming on strong, but am I coming on like a ho? I just want to make sure he knows I'm interested."

"No Rita, he's a hard catch. Keep on he'll break eventually."

"You'll put in a good word for me?"

"I got you this job didn't I? Of course I will."

"Thanks," as Rita hugged Bordeaux he wished he was twenty-five years younger; but he asexually absorbed the hug and watched the beautiful young lady walk down the hall away from the captain's office."

"I promise I won't say a word," mocked Ben as Bordeaux caught him in the stairwell heading up to the captain's office.

"I won't."

"Damn it Bordeaux, stop encouraging her."

"Who says I'm encouraging her?"

"You're supposed to be a detective…you should know by now Rita isn't my type."

"How do you know? She might be…Ben she's a good girl, I've known her and her family all her life…I know she's a little showy, but she's a good Christian girl."

"A good Christian girl? Are you kidding me?" Ben looked at his partner with mild amusement.

"So hook up with her…what could it hurt?"

"You…know…she's…not…my…type."

"Oh horse-feathers, you aren't old enough to know what your type is. Trust me Rita is your type if you'd give her a chance."

"You know you're incorrigible, right?"

"Well I told her I'd put in a good word for her."

"Okay, okay…you've put in your good word, let it go?"

"Not a chance. Maybe one day…"

"But not anytime soon?"

"Nope."

"You know I'm in a relationship."

"There is a difference between a relationship and a dalliance."

Chapter Three

The killer wore a rough brown robe. On bended knee, head to the ground the killer appeared to be a fourteenth century monk, or possibly a priest; however the killer was not a monk, nor had the killer ever been a clergyman of any organized religion. This didn't mean the killer wasn't religious, religion or rather God had brought the killer to this point. A casual observer could have believed the killer was tempting God or merely being facetious, but this killer was dedicated, a true believer.

Submissively the killer began to pray:

"The Lord is my Shepard; I shall not want. He maketh me to lie down in bloody fields. He leads me beside the troubled waters. He DAMNED my soul. He drives me in the path of wickedness against his names sake. Yea, though I walk through the valley of the shadow of death, I will fear no evil; for I am evil and none may harm me. My sword is my weapon against the coming of the righteous. The Lord prepares a table before me in the presence of my enemies and anoints me with the blood of the innocent. My cup runs over with the blood of the slain.

Though I am unworthy I pray my lord your mercy follow me in spite of the things I do. Please Lord remove this burden; I have seen enough death. Let these burdens pass from me if only for a while. I pray Lord: Take this offering, smell the sweet flesh of my sacrifice to you and heed my prayers. I ask you accept this sacrifice as an admission of guilt and a gift from your valiant servant. Let this cup pass from my lips. I ask these things in the name of your son The Christ born of the virgin mother, Amen.

"Amen," came a voice from behind the killer.

Without bothering to turn around, the killer said, "Hello Michael, glad you could make it to the cleansing."

"This is wrong Azrael."

"How can an entity who has done no wrong know the difference? You've always done the right thing Michael, you are one of the chosen. If you wish to speak to me call me by my given name."

"The name Father gave you is Azrael. You know this is wrong, you need to get back to your job. This diversion from your duties angers the council."

Azrael whirled around to face Michael drawing the *Angel's Sword,* "Diversion?" Azrael asked, as the angel's eyes became flaming embers, "what would you know of diversions? You were always one of the perfect ones, one of the beloved while I am an outcast unable to bask in the love of the Father! As for your *Council of Angels*, they govern me not, their sphere of influence does not include me Brother."

"Put your sword away Azrael, you know you can't threaten me, you are not my equal in battle. I am Father's right hand, his weapon. Azrael, I know the master plan; this digression isn't part of Father's plan. If you keep this up, they will come for you Azrael. Please Azrael do not anger Father further."

"Master Plan, there is no plan except death and destruction. These humans die of everything and nothing, if dying of disease and hunger weren't enough, they constantly design new ways to kill each other. Plan? What Plan? Years ago Father damned me with this...abomination. Do you understand, I've been killing people for an eternity? This is my job, my job is to kill people."

"No...Azrael, you are to assist the inhabitants of this world during transcendence to the next plane. You are not delegated to murder the followers and their offspring."

"Return to Father, Michael; mind your own business, I know my responsibilities well, I've had a great many years to come to understand them. I need not your counsel and your Council of Angels may try what they wish. I care not."

"Azrael please, Father sent me to you. He instructed me to show you the way. Father demands you do things his way, not yours, he is growing angry by your sacrifices; they are an abomination to him."

"Go away Michael." The killer sheathed the *Angel's Sword* and turned to the bimah inside the large synagogue and resumed the purification process.

Lighting a small fire in a firepot brought into the synagogue for this purpose, Azrael looked down at the small girl bound tightly on the lectern turning the lectern into a makeshift sacrificial altar. *I wish there were another way,* thought Azrael once again removing the antediluvian *Angel's Sword* from its sheath. Standing by the fire the Angel of Death heated the tip of the long narrow blade until it was white hot. With the sword ready, the killer turned to the young girl bound on the makeshift altar and looked directly into her face.

Ignored and not wishing to see the events he knew was coming, Michael left.

The verbal exchange had perplexed and terrified Naomi Jarnigan, but looking up into the face of her would be killer she wasn't afraid. Gazing up into the most beautiful, kindest face she had ever seen, she knew this person would not, could not do a little girl harm. Surely God wouldn't let this person harm her.

As a result the little girl was not afraid as Azrael, *The Angel of Death*, bent down to whisper something in a language the young girl nor anyone else alive today had ever heard in spoken form. Naomi may not have known the words the killer mouthed into her ear, but she understood the meaning of them. Tonight she would be with God. This very night she would be able to speak with the ruler of the cosmos and for the first time, God would speak back to her. Naomi's prayers tonight would get more than his silence.

The killer's words were little comfort as the white hot blade pushed into her left eye. As Naomi's back arched with pain and she struggled mightily against her bonds; the killer continued to push the blade until there was contact with the back of Naomi's skull. The struggle lasted only a moment and the charring brains brought a wisp of sweet smelling smoke as the white-hot sword cooled.

Removing the sword and sheathing it, the killer kissed Naomi as was the custom, breathing in the essence of her personality. Now the little girl was a permanent part of the *Angel of Death.* As the girl's spirit rose out of the shell she had once inhabited, the killer wiped a tear from what had only a moment ago been a dry eye and instructed the little girl's soul on the way to the Heavenly Father, watching as one of the lesser angels came to show the young girl the way.

Certain none of the young girl's spirit remained in the shell, the *Ancient Rites of Passage* began, preparing the body to be received once again by Mother Earth. Cleaning the body in the ancient ways of old, Azrael took great care in the purification rites. Completing this, Azrael took the sword, which had been cooled completely in the blood of the slain, and carved the tender meat from the backbone of the young girl's corpse, placing it on the fire bringing the slightly sweet smell of charring ham. As the fresh meat began to char on the sacrificial fire; the killer began to sing a funeral hymn in a beautiful unearthly voice.

As the sacrifice was now finished, the killer reverently dressed Naomi in a white silk robe and placed her body once again on the large lectern and appreciatively kneeled before the bimah and prayed for Naomi Jarnigan's young soul. Although Azrael was not permitted to enter the Heavenly Gates, the killer knew Naomi was now in a much better place than this foul world.

The killer left the synagogue with no worries, looking at photographs removed from the inside pocket of the coarse brown robe. Though the photos had been taken last summer, the killer knew the girls were now the perfect age for sacrifice and transcendence. Soon Azrael *the Angel of Death* would help them on their way to the Heavenly Father.

The killer addressed an envelope, selected a photo and wrote a short phrase on the back in beautiful handwriting, sealed the photo inside an envelope and walked down to a mailbox and dropped the envelope inside. Soon it would all begin again.

Jaime's Story

Chapter Four

A majestic Red Oak standing in the front yard shed its leaves in anticipation; spring was right around the corner. A brisk wind littered the asphalt drive with the brown saucer-sized leaves from the old soldier which had seen peace and war alike in its brief time upon the earth; soon the five-hundred year old tree would once again look new as the bright green leaves graced an ancient frame.

Jaime Iron took a deep breath of the cool humid air as she studied the loops and whorls written in the bark of the magnificent specimen standing in her front yard. As she attempted to bring the tree to life on her canvas her thoughts strayed to her financial situation. The insurance money was running out. Had it really been eight years since she'd had a job? Time really did fly.

Eight years ago Jaime's pregnancy forced her to take a leave of absence. The pregnancy had been a hard one, so sick she couldn't keep anything on her stomach for more than a few minutes, Jaime spent most of the first three months on the couch, in bed, or kneeling in front of the toilet. As the pregnancy progressed, Dr. Kalee, Jaime's OBGYN warned her something was wrong. In the second trimester, the Dr. found a tumor growing on Jaime's ovary. As the pregnancy progressed the tumor grew to the size of a grapefruit. Inoperable without terminating the pregnancy, Jaime had made an impossible decision.

Although her chances of living were less than one in a thousand and with her husband's protest lodged, Jaime couldn't condemn her babies to death.

Please have the surgery, Arnold had pleaded.

Jaime couldn't do it. They were her babies, and a good Christian woman couldn't kill her daughters. Jaime's chance of living were one in a thousand, but her daughter's chances of living through a surgery to remove the tumor were one in a million. Maybe if she hadn't been so devout she could have terminated the pregnancy; but her religious beliefs forbad the termination of pregnancy even at the cost of her own life.

God must have been on her side, within days of making the decision to remain pregnant the tumor disappeared completely and the rest of her pregnancy had been normal culminating in the birth of identical twin daughters. Dr. Kalee called Jaime's twin girls— Connie Kay and Lavis Ann—the miracle babies.

Only two short years later Arnold lost a brief battle with pancreatic cancer and like so many other mothers; Jaime was left alone to raise the twins.

The girls had started school last year, and Jaime was the quintessential school mom. Nothing would be better in Jaime's eyes than to spend the rest of her daughters' school years as a house mother, able to attend every school function with cookies and smiles; but the money was going to run out in less than two years if she didn't return to work. It was a shame they hadn't purchased enough life-insurance to cover Arnold's income.

Two months ago she had even called her old boss. Roger was eager for Jaime to return; having been a profitable part of his business, but she couldn't imagine driving from Colbert Heights to Huntsville every day. Jaime had been hearing good things about a young lady in Russellville who owned a brokerage, maybe if she gave Lori Sandusky a call, Lori would give a former Real Estate agent a chance to earn at least a part-time income.

The painting was almost complete. As Jaime put the finishing touches on the landscape she noticed the mailman stopping in front of her mailbox. Stan raised his hand in a brief wave of greeting as he drove away in his Chevy Lumina, sitting on the wrong side.

The March wind brought a chill as she walked down the drive. Soon the Bradford Pear trees lining the drive would be in full bloom, maybe by the weekend. Jaime embraced the fresh air and cool breeze which would soon blow in the spring rains. Spring wasn't Jaime's favorite time of the year—it rained too much—but spring came before summer, which was her favorite season.

In a few months, the heat and humidity would arrive in full force in Alabama and the cold chilly days would be forgotten until after Labor Day when the weather would once again begin to cool off. Her heart lifted at the thought of summer. Days at the lake, and driving with the top off the Jeep, the girls in their cute little bathing suits and skinned knees covered in Triple-Antibiotic Ointment. The Iron girls loved summer.

Looking both ways for an errant speeding car before crossing the road to her mailbox, having been born in Mobile, a town which was never completely quiet, Jaime marveled at the stillness of the small town. She wasn't completely sure if the relative silence and slow pace would eventually seem normal, but it didn't seem normal yet. Glancing at her watch, Jaime saw it was almost three. In a little more than twenty minutes Connie Kay and Lavis Ann would bounce from the bus, two bundles of energy who would not be still until they were tucked into bed and Jaime was reading their nightly story.

She opened the mailbox and pulled out the stack of mail. Sale papers and the garbage bill, a catalogue from Fingerhut, and a reminder from Thornton Chrysler Dodge it was time to service her Jeep, then at the bottom of the pile was the very piece of mail the housewife had prayed she would never see.

With trembling hands she turned the envelope over so she could see the beautiful calligraphy. The envelope was light as a feather even if it weighed heavy on her heart—Jaime knew of the killings, there wasn't a mother in the Southeast who didn't. Until now the killings had seemed to be in another world, another reality, far removed from the small community of Colbert Heights, Alabama and Jaime's little piece of the American dream; but here it was, all too real with no return address, mailed from Birmingham two days ago. With shaking hands she opened the envelope, Jaime's heart stopped momentarily as she recognized what was inside. Like all the other mothers who had come before; Jaime prayed she would never receive the snow white envelope with the ethereal calligraphy. Inside was a single photograph of Jaime and her two daughters last year frolicking on the beach at Williams Hollow. The killer must have been within mere feet of them as he snapped the photograph. Turning over the photograph she saw the words she dreaded with every fiber of her being.

Connie Kay and Lavis Ann Iron have been chosen for Transcendence.

"Oh no…Ohmigod," Jaime muttered as she dropped everything except the picture and without looking either way rushed across the road and up her drive to the house to call the police.

Chapter Five

Bordeaux pulled on McElroy's sleeve to stop him in the stairwell. "Hold on a minute," Bordeaux said as he closed his eyes and thought for a minute. "You know the last one, the last girl. We had officers in the motel room with them. We had officers standing outside the door, a whole parking lot full of cops, and this girl like an Old Testament miracle, disappears in the middle of the night. I've been chasing murderers a long time and I've never seen anything like this...for the first time in my career I don't know what to do Ben. I mean tell me what can I do?"

"I have no idea Detective," Ben said.

"Geez, I mean, I've done everything I know. I mean the kids parents were in the room, we had video cameras in the room at the time the last girl disappeared. We've got seven cameras in the room, now we've got seven cameras with four minutes of static during the time of the disappearance. I don't know. I wish I had something I could tell somebody, but I don't. Somehow if this was something good, I'd call it a miracle, and I'm very close to calling it supernatural. I don't know any other way to explain it."

"So now you're going to try to tell me this whole thing is some kind of supernatural event? This is somehow not a human doing this? After two years being your partner this is the dumbest thing I have ever heard you say."

"No, well I don't know what we've got. I'm not trying to say this is a supernatural event. I'm sure this guy isn't superman. Ben for the first time in a very long time, I really don't know how we are missing, what we're missing. Everything we've been trained to do, doesn't seem to work with this guy. How can there be no physical evidence? Why is there four minutes of static instead of video of the abduction? How did this guy walk into the room with a cop and the parents and take this little girl without anyone seeing? Twenty-five dead girls and I am sure there will be twenty-six by this time tomorrow. The last abduction will make twenty-six. Now we have no more evidence than we had when the first abduction happened. We have twenty-five…" Bordeaux trailed off.

"This is the strangest case I've ever seen Detective. How did this guy know we had this family in Birmingham? How could he know?"

"I don't know how he could know, I agree with you about the strange part. Personally I feel as useless as a civilian."

"I know what you mean, and we're not the only ones. There are twenty FBI agents on this case also. We aren't the only two detectives not making the grade here."

"Twenty FBI agents are supposed to make me feel more useful? We're supposed to be the best investigators in the state," said Ben. "Just because the

FBI is involved and supposedly have their best investigators here doesn't mean the people here don't expect us to do our jobs. We've got a reputation here, you know?"

"I know Ben; I know we have a reputation. I also know we have no *evidence...*"

"You don't have to shout at me Detective."

"I'm not shouting at you personally, not intentionally anyway. I'm frustrated."

"I know. Let's go over what we have again."

"All we've got is a profile. You know what it says: White male thirty-five to forty-five, most likely Jewish, possibly Catholic. Nothing else useful in the profile."

"Well we do have the photographs."

"Yeah, the photographs. So far the lab hasn't been able to determine anything about the photographs. According to the science geeks, they have no idea what kind of photographs they are. The method of processing is unknown, as is the manufacturer of the photographic ink and paper. Someone has created a new type of camera and a new process for making photos. We have only one thing the press doesn't know; these photos aren't normal. Which isn't really a lot to go on unless we happen to come upon a new-fangled photo lab."

"Well it's something, something we could certainly use in a trial."

"To have a trial, we have to catch a killer first."

"Catching him is obviously going to be harder than we first expected. He's killed twenty-five girls in as many days. Naomi Jarnigan will be twenty-six."

"I know…she's dead, we'll get the call *Where* she's dead shortly…I still don't get how we…how he could've walked into the motel room and waltzed right out past all of the cops. How'd he do it?

"I don't know Ben, I just don't know."

"What about the families, do they have anything in common?"

"They all go to church every Sunday."

"Anything else?"

"All the girls are the same age, and as you already know they're all from Alabama."

"Which tells us…?"

"The Perp is from Franklin County or the surrounding area."

"He shouldn't be this hard to find. There aren't many Catholic or Jewish people in Franklin County."

"We should have a lead on him by now."

"It'll come soon. He's getting anxious. He called me today."

"Are you kidding me? He called you."

Bordeaux recanted the conversation to his partner.

"So he has your phone number? What did he sound like?"

"Well...he didn't sound like a he...I don't know exactly, but the voice was crystal clear. I think the killer was using a device which disguises your voice...but the cadence somehow didn't sound like a man..."

"Really?"

"Well it took the two of you long enough to get here," Captain Gaines said brusquely.

"Boss, you wanted to see us?"

"Colbert County Sheriff's Department e-mailed me this a few minutes ago. Jaime Iron from Colbert Heights received it earlier today." Captain Gaines slid a photocopy of a woman and two girls across the desk.

"On the back?" asked Bordeaux.

"Was this," the captain slid a facsimile of the back of the photograph across to Bordeaux and McElroy.

"Where's Colbert Heights?"

"North Alabama, Colbert County…head up 65 toward Cullman, I'll have Rita shoot you the directions."

"Copy that, let's go Ben."

The two investigators walked out of the Bureau office to Bordeaux's unmarked Chevy Tahoe. Bordeaux got in on the driver's side and buckled his seatbelt. When Ben was buckled in he backed out of the parking spot and turned on the lights and siren and headed for the interstate. On the interstate he pushed the Tahoe up to one-twenty and within a few minutes Ben had the directions. Forty minutes later he pulled into Jaime Iron's driveway.

Daniel stepped out of the car to a familiar face. It was a face he hadn't seen in a long time, from a time he'd hoped to forget. "Evening Enoch," Daniel said.

"Well…if it ain't Sergeant Bordeaux," said a short frail looking black man. "How ya been Danny boy? I ain't Enoch no more, I'm Ernie now…I changed it when we got back from that hell-hole. I'm just Ernie…that's what everbody called me anyways."

"Ernie huh? I don't recall ever calling you Ernie…" Daniel said contemptuously.

Feeling the tension between the two cops McElroy asked, "You guys know one another?"

"Yeah," both answered.

"We were in country together, this little bastard saved my life," Bordeaux continued. "But that's been a long time ago; more than forty years ago, a forgotten place in a shitty little country no ever heard of till our boys started getting killed over there."

"Doesn't seem that long, does it?" asked the sheriff's investigator.

"I could have stood it if I hadn't seen your ugly black butt for another forty years. What are you doing here anyway? I thought you were in Cali...did you have to run? Some little girl pregnant?" Bordeaux turned to his partner, "He's probably running from some little boy's father...he's got a thing for boys."

"Screw you Bordeaux...Screw you; you were the one with the thing for cute little VC boys...not me!"

"I'd watch him if I was you," said Bordeaux, "you're almost as cute as those VC boys, Ben. However they probably would frown on him taking a shot at you in Colbert County. He's a ruthless little killing machine with almost a hundred confirmed kills...efficiency courtesy of the Marine Corps Sniper School."

"Now you know that's a long time 'hind me. Did my green time, come home and did twenty for LAPD. Now I'm home."

"Retired twice and still wearing a uniform?"

"Yeah, I retired…came home and stayed with momma a few days...and got bored and retarded; so I applied for a job with the sheriff's department."

"And they made you an investigator?"

"What? You don't think a skinny little country nigger can investigate? They learned me a few things since Viet-Nam you ignorant racist bastard."

"Been a long time," Bordeaux pulled the thin black man into a bear hug looking like he would crush the life out of the frail looking old man.

"So did you bring some answers today? This little lady here is scared to death after getting that pitcher. Strangest thing I ever did see."

"Uh-oh," Ben and Bordeaux said in unison, they both knew if the picture was strange it had to be the same guy.

"Tell me about the picture," Bordeaux said.

"It feels like you're watching a movie. It's in 3-D, technology I ain't never seen before. Kids playing on the beach, momma in the background, don't see how it operates…ain't got no place for batt-rees, no SIM cards, thin as a reg'lar piece of paper, but stiff like plastic. Thinnest moving pitcher I ever seen fore."

Bordeaux looked at Ben then back to Ernie slightly puzzled. The deputy was describing something they hadn't seen before. "Are you saying the picture is moving? Like a movie?"

"Yeah, like watchin' a memory. See the girls playing on the beach, in the background can see other people aroun' and birds flyin', waves from the wakes of boats lappin' on the beach, 's'like watching a silent movie where a body walked aroun' and what they see become a pitcher."

"The little girl, is her eyes burned out?" Ben asked the deputy.

"No...girls, two of em, eyes all strange an shit...'peer to be on far. After bein' out yonder," he pointed west, "I thought I'd seen ever-thang, but I ain't never seen no shit like this. This somethin' new, if it's a viewer it's the skinniest thang I've ever seen. It looks just like a pitcher 'cept everbody in it's moving; here look for your ownself." Ernie reached into the Colbert County patrol car and removed a small plastic bag containing one photograph.

Holding up the plastic bag it only took a second to see the photo fit the profile. He turned to Ernie and Ben and said, "We have to get them out of here. If we don't they'll be dead by morning. Come on guys let's move. Ben get me a chopper out here now. I'll give the pilot flight plans when we board."

Jaime stood watching the cop convention which had magically appeared in her front yard. Everywhere were the flashing blues of their patrol cars, lighting up the yard and making bushes, weeds and trees take on a blinking color not found in nature.

Why were they standing out there talking, laughing, and was the big man in the suit hugging the little black deputy? Why didn't they do something for God's sake? Her girls couldn't become twenty-seven and twenty-eight. They have to do something.

Sooner rather than later Jaime heard a light knock at her front door. She opened the door to a strikingly handsome man. Jaime looked appraisingly at the man standing framed by her doorway. He stood about five feet eight inches tall, but seemed taller. He had wide shoulders, the kind of shoulders her father used to call plough-hands shoulders and a trim waist. As he came through the front door she noticed he had to turn slightly sideways to keep his shoulders from rubbing the door frame.

Jaime looked into the rugged face which held hard, steel-grey eyes and no humor; this man had seen little happiness in his life. If the eyes were a window to the soul, this man's life had been hard and joyless. Jaime held his eyes for only a moment before she had to look away, but continued her inspection and appraisal of him. His hair had once been dark but was now salt and pepper with considerably more salt than pepper. She put his age slightly older than her, he was maybe fifty, fifty-one.

"Evening Ma'am, I'm Daniel Bordeaux and this is my partner Benjamin McElroy," he gestured to the effeminate blonde kid behind him, "We're the

investigators assigned to this case by the Alabama
Bureau of Investigation."

"Come on in, I'll get you a cup of coffee," Jaime said.

"No, we don't have time for coffee. Get the girls and
a week's worth of clothes together, chopper will be
here in less than an hour."

"Chopper? Do you mean helicopter?"

"Yeah," Daniel said, "we have to get you and the girls
somewhere safe. This will happen tonight or
tomorrow. So far the girls have all been dead within
forty-eight hours of receiving the photos. We're
moving you to a secure place provided by the witness
relocation program."

Less than an hour later Jaime and her two girls
boarded a government helicopter outfitted to carry
passengers. The girls were excited by the upcoming
helicopter ride, their enthusiasm dampened not one
bit by their mother's dark mood. Connie Kay and
Lavis Ann couldn't quite figure out why they were
going for a helicopter ride, but the reason why didn't
matter nearly as much as the fact they were going.

"Mommy, where we going?" asked Lavis Ann after
they were airborne. "We going to see God? We going
to see Daddy?"

Lavis Ann's questions brought a wave of tears to
Jaime's eyes. This couldn't be happening, could it?
Why would anyone want to kill her girls? Looking

over at her two girls, Jaime could see they were the spitting image of herself at their age. They were tiny, blonde, blue-eyed angels, and she couldn't believe anyone would want to harm something as innocent as two little girls.

"Where are we going?" Jaime asked the brawny investigator. She couldn't remember his name but he looked capable of protecting a pretty lady and her two little girls.

"We're going to fly into Nashville; a Witness Relocation Officer will meet us there. From there I have no idea. There will be no way anyone will be able to find us. It would be a miracle if anyone found us."

Chapter Six

The killer watched as the two little girls and two adults boarded the helicopter. Azrael really didn't care where they were going, finding them would not be a problem. Right now the killer had other things to do. As the helicopter ascended Azrael stood within feet of the closed doors, oblivious to the dirt and small stones tossed into the air by the whirring blades of the chopper.

Azrael sat on the hill overlooking the motel the police had sequestered the Iron family in; as if hiding them would help. Humans, so intelligent, yet so dumb. You could leave them all the clues or no clues and they didn't understand sometimes there was nothing to understand. The species was so intelligent, yet they did their best to completely ignore the spiritual world as if ignorance would make it simply go away.

Humans wanted to explain everything with science, forensics, geology, biology, chemistry, mathematics, but they missed the understanding which came with feeling and knowing you were part of something bigger than the seen and easily explainable. Science would never explain how a sterile woman became pregnant or where the human soul was hiding. Almost any scientist would tell you the more they discovered the less they knew. Every discovery brought only more questions.

Why were these people so dead set on explaining away God? Why were they so certain God was a fictitious being of legend? Father was as real as any of these humans, more so considering God's wish could make it as if the human never existed. With a single thought God could make any of his creations disappear as if they were a gentle fog dissipating under a noon day sun.

God had shown his might to these little people over and over and within a single generation they were once again unbelievers. These humans wanted everything to be a cosmic accident. Azrael had lived so long with the understanding Father was the supreme being; the angel couldn't possibly come to an understanding why or rather how anything could believe life on earth was a random accident. Once upon a time Azrael had been mortal, once Azrael had been ignorant as to the workings of the universe, but there had never been a time in which Azrael hadn't believed in God.

Azrael's position as one of the Archangels made Azrael more powerful than a human could ever understand, the Archangel understood an angel's power derived from God's will, and The Father could replace Azrael with a single thought. Of all the angels only Gabriel and Michael were Azrael's equal, but were prevented from interfering as they held a different place in the heavenly court.

Only one Angel was greater than Azrael, The former Angel of Light, was the greatest of all the angels, with a power rivaling The Father's. Because of a family quarrel long before Azrael's time, The Advocate, Lucifer had been cast down into darkness and walked the earth freely. Some days he was Azrael's only friend.

Azrael only wanted to be in the heavenly court and would gladly trade all the power to be the lowliest of the choir angels if it allowed Azrael to bask in the glow of the Heavenly Father. Azrael was not permitted to enter the gates of heaven, the only angel not permitted to enter heaven. Even Lucifer the Advocate was allowed to enter the Heavenly Kingdom so long as he wore the attire of an angel proper, but not Azrael. So long as Azrael held the job as the Supreme Angel of Death it was not permitted Azrael should enter into the Kingdom. Azrael could only feel the love of Father when God ventured forth into the wilderness. Jealousy was the only feeling Azrael had left, jealousy and anger.

Soon the day would come, the day when this burden was lifted, the day when no longer would Azrael be the unwilling servant forced to remain in the wilderness because of a mistake millenniums ago, a mistake which happened in a time before the current human occupants of earth began to measure time.

Touching the *Angel's Sword*, Azrael was instantly transported to the motel room in which the Iron women were sequestered.

Azrael watched Jaime Iron sleep with her twin girls. It was time; Connie Kay Iron's time was short. Very soon Connie Kay would grace the sacrificial fire. Azrael climbed into the bed with the two Iron girls and Jaime Iron. Azrael lay for a moment in the bed wondering how it would feel to have a family. It had been so long since Azrael had known what a family life was like. Being a loner in the appointed job, the only family Azrael had now—*The Council of Angels*—mostly shunned Azrael as if Azrael's evil could rub off on them. Rarely did they feel like family, the only angels who even bothered to speak to Azrael were Michael, Gabriel and The Advocate. Rarely did Azrael feel like the *Council* was family. The Council held no love for Azrael, and they should, wasn't the job of family to love you when you were unlovable? The only time Azrael felt loved was in the presence of The Father. Although God's love was unconditional, it was easy to forget when Azrael was forced to be *The Angel of Death.*

I want to be loved again like the Iron girls, thought Azrael. *All I want is to be loved.*

Azrael brushed Jaime's cheek with fingers bearing long glossy nails. Jaime didn't deserve the tribulations which were coming her way, but who deserved to live through the death of a child? Azrael could feel the fear coming from the twin's mother; Jaime had survived the death of her husband, and was now terrified she was losing her girls. Jaime's fear was not unfounded, she was going to lose her two girls and there was nothing anyone or anything could do about it. Only God could intervene to save the life of the two girls and God had never interfered before. Regardless what Michael said, God seemed content to let Azrael do the job assigned, knowing the children would soon be with him in a much better place.

Silently without even rustling the covers Azrael lifted Connie Kay from between her mother and sleeping sister. There was not enough movement to disturb even the hyper-aware mother. Azrael turned one last time before walking through the door to the balcony of the motel room.

Connie Kay woke suddenly and looked at the beautiful figure holding her. Connie felt she should be afraid of the being holding her; however she found it impossible to be afraid of the beautiful, kind face she saw. Azrael whispered something into Connie Kay's ear and the little girl nodded in agreement. "Mommy...I love you...I'm going to be with God tonight. I love you Mommy. Try not to be sad when I'm gone. Mommy I'll see you before you know it. Bye Mommy...I love you."

Jaime awoke to see Connie Kay being held by a tall imposing man. The door to the motel room was open and the figure was walking out with Connie Kay looking over his shoulder. "Bye Mommy, I love you," Connie Kay said as the motel room was shut silently by the tall stranger.

Jaime leaped from the bed screaming, "He's got my girl, somebody do something…He's got my girl…Daniel get him, he's got my girl," Jaime rushed out onto the balcony watching as the stranger walked quietly down the stairs.

Daniel Bordeaux woke with screaming in his ear. Jaime Iron was beating on his door screaming like there was no tomorrow. Daniel leaped from the bed pausing only a minute to put on a pair of trousers lying on the nightstand. As Daniel entered the other motel room he saw Jaime Iron standing in only a t-shirt with one of the girls pulled close to her. The other was nowhere to be seen.

"Don't stand there with a stupid look on your face, get the man who took my girl. He walked out of the door holding her…she said I love you Mommy as he walked out with her."

"When," asked Daniel.

"Just now. He should be in the parking lot now."

Daniel rushed out of the door to see a Tennessee trooper toward him at the end of the steps. "What's going on," asked the trooper. "I thought I heard someone screaming."

"Ms. Iron has been screaming her head off, someone took one of the girls."

"Impossible; I've been watching the door the whole time. No one has been in or out of her room all night. I came running when she started to scream. There hasn't been anyone up on the second floor in more than an hour. Sure the little girl didn't go to the bathroom?"

"No, she said she watched a man carry the little girl out the door. She said the girl spoke to her before the man closed the door."

"Impossible. I was watching the door the whole time. The only person who has come out of Ms. Iron's door tonight was Jaime Iron and you!"

"All right genius? Where is the little girl?" asked Bordeaux. "Did she evaporate? Did Mr. Scott beam her up? There are two ways into room 226, through the front door, or through my room and the only door to my room sits six inches from Ms. Iron's door. You were asleep trooper. Get me a report from the perimeter guards.

Daniel listened as the guards in the parking lot one by one answered on the radio. Each one checked in, reporting nothing unusual. "No one has seen a thing sir," said the trooper.

"I heard very well trooper…Get everyone looking for the perp. I want a net up around this motel, ten miles check every vehicle; I mean I want *every vehicle checked*! I want officers around the perimeter checking under every bush and behind every blade of grass. I want the helicopter in the air. I want anyone on foot checked. Come on guys, let's go; wake everyone."

Daniel turned and walked back to Jaime's room. Opening the door, Daniel saw Jaime sitting on the edge of the bed tears staining her beautiful face. She held the remaining girl close to her breast hugging her tightly as her tears ran into the little girl's hair, darkening the girl's blonde hair slightly where the tears fell. If she hadn't been so distressed, she would have been beautiful; she was beautiful. As Daniel pushed the door closed behind him she looked up her blue eyes glistening with tears and her face red and puffy from her tears.

Jaime spoke as she looked up, her face hopeful, "Did you find Connie Kay?"

"No, but we will. Every cop in Tennessee is looking right now. He won't escape. We'll find him. We've got out an Amber alert, every car moving within 20 miles will be checked. Now I need to ask you a few questions."

"I don't know what help I can be, but I'll try."

"Ok, tell me what the perp looked like."

Jaime looked confused, "What's a perp?"

Daniel felt a moment of fear. He knew they had let a killer slip through their fingers. This girl was gone, this detail was too big; there was a leak somewhere. Someone was telling the perpetrator where they were hiding, but how could he get into the room and leave without being seen. Daniel made a decision, *have to get them out of here,* he thought. *This time it will only be me and the Federal Man. I won't even tell the captain where I'm taking them.*

Chapter Seven

Jaime slept fitfully in the new motel room's bed with her remaining daughter. Daniel had dragged Jaime and Lavis Ann here after the abduction of Connie Kay.

Suddenly without warning the motel room filled with light waking her up. She rubbed her eyes sleepily as she sat up in the bed and looked at a figure which seemed to be lit internally, as if he were a source of light.

The figure seemed to be male and was much larger than any human had right to be. This (man?) had to be at least nine feet tall and was twice as broad across the shoulders as any man Jaime had ever seen. Jaime looked at the figure and saw features which could be considered male or female. There was the strong jaw line and wide shoulders of a man, but the flawless skin and manicured nails of a woman. When the figure spoke there was no doubt this being was inherently male.

"You have to leave this place," boomed the deep male voice.

"Who, what…are you?" asked Jaime with a shaky voice.

"I am Michael, The Champion."

"Champion?" Jaime questioned.

"God's Champion, his Right Hand, and guardian of the people. I am Gods Weapon against the demons who will not go quietly into the darkness. I am the General of **The One True God's Army!**"

"The one true God?"

"Yes, the heavenly father. Who I am is not the reason I am here. You and your daughter are in danger. I cannot protect you here. You must return home as Azrael is coming for the remaining daughter. The child is special, she must not be taken."

"What is Azrael?"

"Azrael is *The Angel of Death*."

"You said you were the Guardian, can you not stop him?"

"I may not. Azrael is one of the most powerful angels in the heavenly court, I am Azrael's equal, but God prevents me from interfering with Azrael. Azrael is allowed to take anyone the *Angel of Death* deems worthy of a place at God's side. I hold no influence and may not interfere directly with Azrael's duties."

"So how can you protect me? If he is as powerful as you describe, nothing can save me."

"God has instructed me to place a protective shield over your home and grounds. So long as you and your child are within the grounds, she may not be harmed."

"What about me?"

Azrael isn't interested in you. You are not yet worthy. God has other plans for you at this time."

"What plans?"

"I know not the mind of the Heavenly Father. I am his Champion; I do not question him or his motives, those duties fall to Lucifer, the advocate. God makes his will known in good time."

"So I have to return home?"

"Yes, you need to return immediately; I have for a short time extended my protection to the police car sitting in the parking lot. None of the persons making this place your prison will be able to remember your passage after you are gone. Leave immediately as my protection of the car will expire with the coming of the dawn."

From beneath his robe Michael brought out a long package wrapped in a pure white material with gold threads running through it. "You will need this sometime in the future. It is a weapon against Azrael. Protect your child. You need to return to your home before the sun comes over the eastern horizon."

Jaime took the package handed to her by Michael. It was heavy and as she unwrapped the package she found a sword of unusual beauty encased in a jeweled sheath. As Jaime removed the sword from the sheath, it glowed with a pale blue light which came from within the fine steel of the sword. "Oh my...I can't...I ...don't think I can."

"Jaime, you don't have a choice. If you don't defend Lavis Ann, the girl will die."

"But why a sword? Could you have given me a gun, or a bazooka or something…anything else?"

"No. This is a traditional weapon, the only weapon which can be used to kill an Angel. If you intend to save your daughter, you must kill the Angel Azrael. Wear the sword at all times. This sword carries the Power of God, so it will be light as a feather as you wear it and no one but you will know you are armed. To kill Azrael you will need to sever the angel's head from the shoulders. Only this will end Azrael's reign as the *Supreme Angel of Death.*"

"If Azrael does manage to take the child, you need only grasp the hilt of the sword and think of Lavis Ann, you will be immediately transported to the location where your daughter is held, hopefully before the child dies. Beyond these things I can offer no more protection. So long as you hold the sword in your hand, neither Azrael nor any being earthly or spiritual may harm you except in a direct battle. If you try to kill Azrael and do not succeed in removing the angel's head, Azrael is allowed to defend. You may be severely injured or killed in a direct conflict with Azrael, remember Azrael has been the *Angel of Death* for untold millenniums and has seen every manner of death imaginable. Unless you are a direct threat you have the protection of God through the Son. You are invincible so long as you grasp the hilt without malice. Take your daughter before the two policemen awaken." Michael produced a ring with a single key, "Here is the key to their car, leave now."

Michael's light faded and the next thing Jaime knew she was lying beside Lavis Ann. The motel room was dark and she could hear the sound from the streets below. Jaime reached over and clicked on the lamp beside the bed.

Waking Lavis Ann quietly, Jaime impressed on the child the need for silence. Daniel Bordeaux and the Witness Relocation man were lying in the room next door, the connecting door between the two rooms was open and she quietly closed the door on her side. When she had finished dressing herself and Lavis Ann, Jaime packed their meager belongings into the suitcase she brought from home. *Why am I doing this,* she wondered, *it was only a dream, it must have been a dream, it couldn't be real. Angels in my dreams; as if!*

Nevertheless as Jaime finished packing she looked over at the bureau provided by the motel and on top of the bureau was a ring with one key on it, and a beautiful jewel encrusted sword. It had been real. An angel named Michael had really visited her with instructions. Picking up the sword she noticed a light belt running through the back of the scabbard.

Jaime wrote Daniel a quick note, belted the sword on, and carried their meager belongings and Lavis Ann out to the car. As she walked the sword at her hip was as light as a feather. Belting Lavis Ann into the front seat, she started the State Police cruiser and backed out of the parking space and drove out of the motel parking lot. In a few minutes she was driving south on I-65 and by the time Daniel Bordeaux awoke Jaime was pulling into her driveway in Colbert Heights Alabama.

Daniel Bordeaux is going to be pissed, Jaime thought. *When he awakes and I'm not there he is going to have a come-apart.* Jaime felt slightly uncomfortable about effectively stealing a state police car, and she knew she didn't want to be anywhere close when Daniel found her missing. She was going to miss the too serious almost somber policeman…who knew, maybe she'd see him again though. She didn't exactly think this was over.

Jaime got Lavis Ann out of the car and turned to walk in the house carrying her young daughter. Lavis looking over her mother's shoulder watched in wonder as the Tennessee State Trooper car disappeared as if it had never been there. This was some kind of trip they were coming back from.

As Jaime Iron drove the last few miles to Colbert Heights, Daniel Bordeaux awoke. He knew without looking at the clock it was five-thirty. Turning on the light next to his bed he looked over at the sleeping federal agent. The man was almost as old as Daniel, but where Daniel was hard and cynical, the federal agent was soft. Daniel had seen far too much death and pain in his time on earth, he'd spent his nineteenth and twentieth birthdays in a shitty little hell hole ten thousand miles from Alabama. The Witness Protection agent had seen none of this, *look at him lying there sleeping like a fattening hog. Fifteen minutes till six and the lazy prick lays there like there isn't a care in the world,* Daniel thought.

Daniel got out of the bed and lit a Marlboro. He'd been trying unsuccessfully to quit for the past forty years, but it was his one vice. As he smoked the cigarette he pulled on a pair of running shorts and went into the small bathroom in the corner of the motel room.

Returning to the bedroom portion of the motel room he finished his cigarette and put on a pair of Nike running shoes. Man how running shoes had changed since his time with the Marines. After Daniel finished tying his shoes he removed a t-shirt from a *Colstrip Discount Store* bag. He hadn't had time to pack a bag, as a result the State of Alabama had bought him necessities.

Daniel opened the door to the motel room, noticing as he did the door to Jaime's adjoining room had been silently closed. He figured she needed a little privacy. He walked out onto the balcony and slammed the door loudly. Maybe the slamming door would awaken the snoring federal agent. Standing on the balcony he did a few warm-up stretches. With his leg on the balcony rail leaning his body into his leg stretching out his hamstring Daniel looked out over the rail.

The car is missing, he thought. The patrol car Daniel and the Iron girls had driven to the new motel was not in the parking space. Daniel stared at the empty parking space momentarily stunned. "She wouldn't have," he muttered under his breath, "surely she has more sense." No, she couldn't have she didn't have a key to the patrol car.

Daniel walked down the stairs twisting slightly to stretch his muscles. When he reached the bottom of the stairs he realized he must have been mistaken. The THP patrol car was sitting right where it supposed to be. The ABI investigator walked around the cruiser. He must have overlooked the car. Daniel lay his hand on the hood of the car, it was warm…he looked up at the balcony at his motel room door, then back at the car. How could he have missed something as big as a patrol car when he was standing no more than twenty feet from it? Shrugging his shoulders in bemusement he jogged through the parking lot and down the street. He needed to get in five miles in the next 30 minutes, so he set off at a rapid pace.

Chapter Eight

Jaime stood at her window and watched as the sun came over the eastern horizon. Standing at the edge of her property line stood a figure in a heavy brown cloak. As Jaime watched the figure he walked around the edge of her property always standing outside the line as if he couldn't cross over.

Jaime walked out of the kitchen, "You stay here," she told Lavis Ann, "I'll be right back." She walked across the yard to the figure standing at the edge of her property. "Who are you?" she asked, "Are you Azrael, are you the angel of death…did you come to take my little girl?" she screamed. "Are you the bastard who murdered my little girl…*Did you take my Connie Kay,* she sobbed. Did you take my Connie Kay…DID YOU TAKE MY CONNIE KAY," she screamed. "Answer me Son of Satan; did you come to take my remaining girl? Did you? Answer me before I kill you like the dog you are."

Azrael turned to Jaime and pulled the cloak back to reveal the face. For the first time in recorded history a person who was not scheduled to die saw the face of the *Supreme Angel of Death*. Jaime had expected the Angel to be disfigured or even ugly; she had expected a figure like the Grim Reaper, a skeleton figure holding a scythe. She expected everything except what she saw.

Death isn't ugly, she thought as Azrael shrugged off the brown cloak and revealed herself to the Iron woman in her full glory. Free from the hood, Azrael shook out her long dark hair. Azrael spread her wings which glittered with gold and green flecks. *Death isn't ugly at all, Death is beautiful, and if this is the Angel of Death she is truly beautiful.* Azrael smiled beautifully, showing a perfect set of even white teeth. If the Angel had been a woman she would have men walking into walls all over town.

"Hello Ms. Iron. I am Azrael. Normally none who sees me is allowed to survive. However you have been granted a reprieve by the Heavenly father for a short time. The reason is not yet known to me, but soon I will come for you and your precious daughter. Soon, within a fortnight your precious Lavis Ann will cook over my sacrificial fire as did her sister this very morning. Your pitiful protector Michael cannot prevent this, tell him when he returns his protection is not enough. I am coming for you sweetheart. I will not be denied."

Jaime suddenly remembered the sword belted at her side and in a fluid motion she drew the sword and plunged it into the breast of Azrael. The Angel's wings which had been folded neatly behind her flared open and stiffened. Azrael's face changed from a gentle smiling face into a mask of horror as thousands of souls rolled across her brightly shining eyes, and then she began to scream. Azrael screamed a blood-curdling unearthly sound no one on earth had ever heard.

Suddenly the scream was inside Jaime's head, the misery of the millions taken by Azrael turned to liquid and blood began to run out of Jaime's ears. All Jaime could think to do was cover her ears. She had to stop the screaming, had to stop the crying, the misery of the slain was leaking out of her ears. Jaime fell backwards and as she did the sword pulled from the Angel's breast and Jaime dropped it on the ground as she covered her ears in a useless attempt to keep the screaming out and the misery in.

When the sword was removed from Azrael's breast, the screaming stopped and Azrael once again stood in her full glory before Jaime. The smile Azrael had earlier was gone now. It was replaced by the naked look of pure un-adulterated anger. "So, I see you have an *Angel's Sword*. Did *The Beloved One* not tell you how to use it? I may not be killed this way; you may only kill an angel by separating the head from the shoulders. Sweet Jaime, like all your kind you don't pay attention to the details, but knowing you have a weapon I will not make the mistake of underestimating you again. So how do I punish you sweet Jaime? The Father says I may not take you at this time, but he has said nothing about your village. Your village will pay the price for your insubordination. The people of Colbert Heights will all soon be dead. Everyone you know will die this very day." Azrael disappeared.

Jaime struggled to pick herself up off the ground as the angel faded. Her head was so sore, reaching up she touched her jawline and felt the wetness of the liquid which had come from her ears. She could only think of it as the misery of the slain. Even now she could still feel the misery which had come with Azrael's scream.

Looking at the sword lying on the ground she bent and picked it up replacing it in the scabbard. It was light as air and she barely felt the weight of it hanging at her hip. Jaime silently cursed herself for making the mistake. Michael had clearly told her she could only kill and angel by separating the head from the shoulders, how had she forgotten such a simple thing. Jaime knew she'd made a mistake, but would Azrael really hold her mistake against the people of Colbert Heights? Would God allow it?

Jaime knelt on the ground and began to pray. *"Our Father which art in heaven, hallowed be thy name, thy kingdom come thy will be done, on earth as it is in heaven. Give us this day our daily bread, and forgive our trespasses as we forgive those who trespass against us. Lead me not into temptation, but deliver me from evil. For thine is the Kingdom, the Power, and Glory forever."* Jaime stood from her position of subservience, as she stood she began a talk with God as she sometimes did, *"Father please protect me and mine. Please remember I am your loyal servant and will bend to your wishes whatever they may be. I know your wish is law and will abide by your decisions. Please Lord protect my daughter, watch over Lavis Ann as if she were your child, which she is. Please Lord I need Lavis Ann...She is all I have left of the man I loved. Lord I need her, sometimes my girls have been the only thing anchoring me to reality when the voices speak to me in the darkness. They are my sanity in this cruel world. Lord if it is as Azrael said and Connie Kay is no longer of this world; please look after her with the gentleness of a mother. Lord I try to live my life as you wish, which because of the things you ask of me can be hard sometimes. I ask for your protection, your grace and your wisdom in this time of tribulation. In the name of your son my savior Jesus Christ, Amen."*

Chapter Nine

Daniel returned from his morning run relaxed and ready for a brand new day. The federal man was up and had showered and brought Daniel a cup of coffee from the lobby.

"Heard anything from next door?" Daniel asked.

"No, it's been quiet over there. We're in a good place, no one knows we're here except the two of us. We'll let them sleep, I know it's been trying for them. It's going to get worse soon. They found the little girl."

"Oh man…where?" asked Bordeaux.

"The West End Synagogue in Nashville."

"Shut the front door…" Daniel ran his hands through his hair and walked over to his night table, picked up a Marlboro and lit it with the Zippo he'd brought back from Saigon. The design had long ago worn away, but the lighter worked as well now as it had way back then. Taking a long pull on the cigarette he looked at the Witness Protection guy and asked, "You have any idea how we were found?

"No…I'm thinking someone told where we were, I wish I knew who it was…I'd see they spent a few years in Hazleton, West Virginia."

"Yeah, I thought about it while I was running. I doesn't make sense. I can't make any sense out of it. The girl disappeared with twenty cops watching her? How does a little girl disappear when twenty cops paid to watch…see nothing?" Daniel took a long drag from the Marlboro and crushed it out in the ashtray, "I'm going to jump in the shower, care to wake up the Ms. Iron? We'll go get breakfast and figure out what to do now."

"Yes, go ahead with your shower, I'll wake them after I walk down and get another cup of coffee. Want one?"

"Nah, I'm good, too much caffeine jingles my nerves too bad."

"Ok I'll be right back."

Bordeaux stripped off his shirt and picked up the razor and shaving cream he'd bought at the Colstrip Discount Store. He shaved and turned on the shower and waited until the water was the correct temperature. He quickly showered and was putting on his rumpled suit when the federal man returned with coffee.

"I'll wake them," Daniel said, "take a while and enjoy your coffee, I'm sure it will be a while before they're ready."

Daniel gently knocked on the door adjoining the two motel rooms. "Ms. Iron? You awake Ms. Iron?" he questioned through the door.

There was no response, so he gently opened the door as he knocked again. "Ms. Iron, are you awake yet. I'm coming in, so make yourself decent." He knocked on the door again and gently opened it to find the motel room dark. The light from the adjoining room spilled inside enough for Daniel to realize the room was deserted. He pushed the door completely open and walked into the room, finding neither the mother nor the child.

Walking back into the room he shared with the federal man, he asked, "Did you see Ms. Iron down in the lobby?"

"No…why isn't she in her room?" the federal man followed Daniel into Jaime Iron's room.

Daniel turned on the light and his eyes immediately went to the note lying in the middle of the made bed.

Before he picked up the note he dropped his head into his large right hand and pinched the bridge of his nose. This case from beginning to end had been a complete logistical nightmare. He had a feeling this note lying in the middle of the bed wasn't going to help things any.

Detective Bordeaux,

I am truly sorry, but I had to leave you in the middle of the night. Michael came to me and told me it wasn't possible for you to protect me here so far from my home. Sorry I had to take the car, but it will be at my house, I'm sure someone can come get it. I am thankful for all you have tried to do and I know you only wanted to protect me and my girls. However after having a discussion with Michael I don't believe you can and he has convinced me to return home.

Yours in Christ

Jaime Iron

Daniel handed the note to the Witness Relocation man as he said, "Un-believable."

Chapter Ten

Daniel Bordeaux was getting angrier by the minute as he sped down I-65. *Damn this woman! All the things the various states had done to protect her and she disappears in the middle of the night? What was she thinking? Stupid Civilians, I wish we could induct all of them in to the Marines for a few weeks so I could at least yell at them without them bursting into tears. Idiot Civilians, can't tell them nothing*

Officer Dale Albrecht sat in his car drinking a cup of lukewarm coffee as the dark blue sedan flew by the beginning of the construction zone at an incredible speed. Looking at his radar Albrecht saw the idiot was running one-oh-six Albrecht may have given the guy five or ten miles per hour over the posted forty-five…but a hundred, no he couldn't allow them to drive through his construction zone at a hundred and six miles per hour.

In his rearview mirror Daniel saw the city car pull out and turn on the blue lights. Daniel reciprocated by lighting up the blue lights on the car provided by the Tennessee Highway Patrol. Seeing the lights in the back window come on, the Davidson County patrolman turned off his lights and slowed his cruiser to a safe speed.

Daniel was only able to maintain his speed for a moment before the traffic was too heavy. Soon even the state patrol car could only travel a maximum of thirty miles an hour. Daniel cursed at the traffic and after a little while wasn't sure if his lights and siren were helping or hurting his progress.

When Daniel finally reached the open road again he looked at his watch; nine o'clock. Fourteen miles in thirty minutes, with blue lights and siren, but now the dark blue cruiser was loping down the road with gazelle like intensity, eating up the final hundred-fifty miles in less than an hour and a half.

As Daniel drove down the interstate, he didn't notice the blooming azaleas, nor did he notice the beautiful shade of light green as the spring approached and made everything look new. His body did recognize the coming of spring as his allergies kicked into high gear, making his nose run and his eyes water.

As Daniel drove up into the driveway of Jaime's home, he did notice the huge oak standing in Jaime's yard had put out fresh new leaves for what had to be the five-hundredth time. The tree was huge, dominating the whole yard, and he thought it would be around for many years after he and everyone else on this planet was long gone if only it was left alone.

Even Daniel's appreciation for the statuesque old tree didn't quell his anger toward Jaime. Nothing short of a miracle could save her from his wrath at this moment in time. Daniel had some things to say to her. None of what Daniel had to say was going to be very pretty or eloquently said. Daniel's anger though sometimes hidden right under the surface was a force to be reckoned with.

Daniel strode up to the door and knocked with a heavy hand. Jaime opened the door looking tired and disheveled. "Come in Mr. Bordeaux, I guess I've got some explaining to do," she said.

"You're damned right you have some explaining to do. How in the hell am I . . . are we supposed to protect you if you don't follow instructions? What in God's name were you thinking? Or were you thinking? This ain't a game lady, this is the real deal. There really is a guy out there who wants to kill your little girl. Not Connie, she was found dead this morning in West End Synagogue in Nashville. Do you understand how serious this is?"

At the mention of Connie's name Jaime burst into tears and collapsed into a heap on the floor at Daniel's feet. "No, No…not my Connie Kay. Where…When…did they…Who found her?" Jaime had known Connie Kay was dead, Azrael had as much as said it, but she hadn't wanted confirmation this way. Jaime had wanted to go on believing in her heart and mind her darling little girl was still alive. Now this man, this hateful man had destroyed her illusion. Why did he have to destroy her illusion?

Daniel's anger cooled rapidly when Jaime collapsed. He hadn't really meant to scream it at her. What was he thinking? No one wanted to find out their child was dead by having a brute of a cop yell it at them while standing in the doorway. Deaths should be handled in a compassionate manner. Even after years of being the deliverer of bad news, he still didn't know how to break it to people their loved ones were dead, but he knew yelling it at them while standing in their doorway wasn't the way a loving mother should find out her seven year old girl was dead. "I'm sorry Ma'am, I was…I'm sorry."

Jaime looked up, her face streaked red from the crying; mascara was running down her face making her look like a bizarre circus clown. "You're sorry? You're sorry? You son-of-a-bitch, how dare you come back here screaming at me. You haven't…you haven't earned the right to yell at me, so don't come in here with your…do you think a badge gives you the right to speak to me like I'm a red-headed stepchild? Get out. Get out."

"Ma'am I…"

"Get out. Get the *fuck out of my house!*"

The words coming out of Jaime's mouth shocked Daniel. He had only known Jaime for a few short days, but in the brief period of time he thought he knew her well enough to know gratuitous profanity was not her usual vocabulary. Jaime Iron was a lady, and as such she conducted herself in a lady-like manner. However right now she seemed as angry as some of the trailer-trash he had dealt with in the past. "Ma'am I'm sorry, you're right I should be more sympathetic. However you should have notified me before you disappeared in the middle of the night. I can't protect you and your little girl if I don't know where you are."

"You don't understand there isn't a thing you can do to protect me and my little girl regardless of where we are." Jaime was now standing looking Daniel Bordeaux directly in the eye. "There's not a thing you or anyone else can do to protect Lavis Ann and I from Azrael."

"Protect you from whom? Where did you hear the name Azrael? Do you know this guy? Do you know who the killer is? Tell me . . . I'll have him picked up."

"You don't understand you can't have her picked up. You don't have the authority. Her authority comes from God not man. There's nothing you or any other human on earth can do to protect Lavis Ann from the Angel of Death. I am the only one who can be her savior."

Daniel looked at Jaime; he saw an odd passionate look in her eyes. It was a look he was familiar with. Daniel remembered the look from many years ago in a little jungle ten thousand miles from here. Soldiers there had been brainwashed to believe Ho Chi Minh would make their lives better by forcing the western devils out of their beautiful country. The little bastards had believed Uncle Ho was the only answer. Daniel couldn't believe this woman, who had seemed so normal yesterday, would suddenly begin believing in fairy tales. "What do you now believe it's an angel running around killing these little girls? Do you know how crazy you sound? On the basis of your last statement alone, I can have you held for psychiatric review at any local hospital."

"Don't you call me crazy!"

"Are you listening to how this sounds?"

"Daniel, you don't understand. I'm not leaving this house, and right now an army of police officers and the National Guard couldn't make me leave. As long as I am here I have the protection of God. If Lavis Ann leaves the boundaries of the property here she is in danger. As long as Lavis Ann remains inside my property lines Azrael cannot harm her. However you and everyone else in Colbert Heights are in danger. Azrael promised me earlier she would kill everyone in this town for my insubordination."

"Your insubordination? What in God's name are you talking about? Are you saying you spoke with this person?"

"Daniel, try and take a leap of faith here, this is not a person it's an angel. She cannot be caught or harmed by a human. Azrael is God's supreme Angel of Death. When Michael came to me earlier this morning he gave me a brief synopsis of Azrael's place in the heavenly order."

"Now wait a minute, who's Michael?"

"The Archangel Michael. He called himself God's Champion."

"So now you are saying you have met not one angel today but two?"

"Exactly, I'm glad I'm finally getting through to you."

"Lady you're doing anything but getting through to me. If you knew how crazy you sound, you would shut your mouth right now. I'm in a good mind to haul you up to the 400 unit and have you held for psychiatric review."

"No, Daniel you won't. Neither I nor my daughter Lavis Ann will be leaving this property for a long while. As capable as you look, you don't have the ability to protect me or my daughter, not from her. As such I will remain here, and you may do or try anything you damn well please. Now if you want to stay you are more than welcome, if not good day sir."

"Lady, do you understand what you are saying? No, you probably don't you're crazy as a loon. You're coming with me." Daniel reached and took Jaime by the arm. If Daniel had expected a soft woman, it was not at all what he reached and grabbed hold of. Jaime Iron lived up to her name and her arm felt like a coiled steel cable. With a move Daniel didn't think anyone or anything on earth could duplicate, Jaime wrenched her arm out of the grasp of the much larger man. With lightning quick speed she moved her left hand to her waist and the action reminded Daniel of an old western hero fast drawing a long barreled pistol from her waistband. When Daniel looked up she held nothing in her hand, but as she drew her hand across Daniel's arm the flesh parted from the bone with the precision of a surgical cut.

Daniel felt no pain at first. The cut was as clean as a laser incision. Daniel looked at the cut opened in his forearm watching as the cut first oozed a little blood then began to pour blood out onto Jaime's foyer tile. What the hell had she cut him with? He had watched plainly as she drew a line across his arm with an imaginary sword.

"Daniel, the next time you touch me without my permission I'll cut your head completely off. I warned you once neither I nor my daughter are leaving this place for a long time."

Daniel looked at Jaime in shock, not from the blood loss, but from the realization of what she had said. Cut his head off with what? "You're crazy as hell lady. What are you going to cut my head off with? Somehow you must have cut me with a razor, but it won't cut my head off. I have handled people like you for more than forty years. I made a mistake underestimating you the first time I won't make the mistake of underestimating you again." Daniel reached into his back pocket and removed a pair of handcuffs. "I think it's time we took a little ride to the hospital. I need to be sewed up. They will hold you for observation. Lavis will be transferred to a secure location where she can be protected from the killer."

"You don't get it do you? I'm not going anywhere." Jaime moved her hand and arm upward stretching out her hand in the direction of Daniel's throat. Daniel felt the cold steel of a blade against the side of his neck. Daniel looked at Jaime's hand, it was curved as if she held the haft of something, but there was nothing there. Jaime's hand held nothing, yet he could feel the steel against the side of his neck. What kind of trick was this?

Jaime felt the righteous anger grip her, *Daniel Bordeaux you don't get to tell me what to do. Who do you think you are? Do you think I will always be a willing fourteen year old to be cowed and forced to do whatever you wish me to do? I am not a little girl anymore. I killed her when I was fourteen so the woman I am now could be born.* "I'll remove the blade if you agree to hear me out."

"Okay, okay."

Jaime removed the blade and saw the pale look on Daniel Bordeaux's face. He wasn't afraid of her, but he had a look of disbelief on his face. He was getting pale, and Jaime suddenly realized why; he was bleeding, badly. Jaime felt a sudden horror at what she had almost done. She had almost killed a state officer. As she looked down at the blood running into the grout lines between the ceramic tile floor tiles she felt compassion. Daniel Bordeaux meant her no harm.

Daniel was doing what he felt was the best thing, and in normal circumstances his best would have been more than enough. These were not normal circumstances though.

Jaime felt an unexplainable desire to help this bleeding man, and suddenly it was as if she could see into his heart. Jaime was suddenly overcome by a great sadness. It wasn't her sadness. It came from this gruff police officer. As she touched his psyche, she instantly understood why he was sad; he had never known the power of love. She could see in his heart there had been occasions of lust, but he had never known true love. Jaime didn't know how she knew this, but she suddenly knew he had never known the love of a good woman, nor did he know the love of the Savior. An unbeliever, he was one of the lost; Daniel Bordeaux had decided there was no God.

Jaime reached out to his arm—wounded by her blade—feeling the warm blood rush through her fingers, she tried to connect to his heart. Jaime felt the blood pumping out of his arm thinking I have to stop him from bleeding, he's ruining my floor.

Daniel felt a flood of compassion pouring from this woman. Even though he didn't know how or why he felt her compassion he could feel it. He should be feeling compassion for her, not the other way around. Daniel stood there as it seemed like his soul emptied into a chasm of love for which he had nothing with which to compare it to. Daniel had never been loved by anyone, thus he had never loved anyone. This wasn't like a physical attraction however, it was more like suddenly he knew there was something else out there, something which loved him regardless of his shortcomings.

While Daniel's soul was connecting to God through Jaime, inexplicably the wound in his arm healed unbeknownst to Jaime. Daniel felt the wound close up with relief. He looked down to find Jaime's hand grasped around his arm between the wrist and elbow. He watched as magically the wound closed and even the scar faded. A metal rod pushed through his pants leg and clattered to the floor.

The sound of metal clattering onto the floor startled Jaime and she let go of Daniel's arm. When she looked up into his face, he didn't seem quite as cynical or as hard-core as he had been. He also looked different somehow. He looked about ten years younger than he had only moments before.

"Is this yours?" Jaime asked as she bent down and picked up a shiny metal rod with screws in each end.

"I've never seen it before, but it felt like it came out of the front of my leg. It looks like a rod used to mend a broken leg."

"Have you ever had a broken leg?"

"A busted leg is why I'm not still a Marine. I was standing next to a guy who stepped on a land mine in Vietnam, busted my leg pretty bad. See," Daniel pulled up his pant leg to show what should have been a horribly scarred and burnt leg. His leg looked fine though. There was none of the scarring Daniel had lived with for more than three decades. How was this possible? How in God's name? "What the hell did you do to me? What kind of place is this?"

"What do you mean what did I do to you, all I did was touch you. I didn't do anything to you."

"You had to do something to me. First you nearly cut my damned arm off then you heal it up and my leg spits out a steel rod doctors put there during the Vietnam War. I broke my leg years before you were born."

"I didn't do it."

"It isn't…I don't believe…You had to do…Lady, what in God's name did you do?"

"I didn't do anything." Once again feeling threatened Jaime touched the handle of the sword. When she did there was a voice from the air. *With God all things are possible. It is written thou shalt worship the Lord thy God and him only shalt thou serve. Fear not children for it is I The Christ, redeemer of lost souls, come to give peace. Jaime, know thou at this time the little one is with me in luxury. She has the peace only my Father can give. Jaime, you must protect the remaining child as she is special to me.*"

"Whoa…" Jaime and Daniel uttered at almost the same time.

"Mommy?"

Jaime and Daniel spun to see Lavis Ann standing at the end of the hallway rubbing sleep out of her eyes.

"Mommy I heard Jesus in my head—least I think 'twas Jesus. He was in my head saying I'm special I have an especial porpoise here. What's a porpoise Mommy?"

"Honey did Jesus say anything else did it say what the purpose was?"

"I don't know Mommy I'se sleeping see…an I…an I…I heard this man…I think it was Jesus…well maybe it was…in my dreams saying I'm special cuz I have an especial porpoise. Jesus said I would one day lead God's Kids out of the wilderness. Like why are God's kids in the wilderness?"

"Did Jesus say anything else "?"

"Don't think so, but it's gettin' hard to 'member. I don' really member much 'bout it anymore."

"Mommy?"

"Yeah, what is it?"

"Is Connie Kay with Jesus? I think I saw her with Jesus."

"Yeah sweetie I think she is."

"Good. I want her to be with Jesus in heaven, but I miss her though. You miss her Mommy? I think when you're gone to be an angel like Jesus said...I'm gonna miss havin' a sister when you're gone."

"What makes you think I'm going somewhere?"

"I dunno. I think you're gonna go be an angel an forget about me, but that's okay 'cause Mr. Bordeaux will take care of me. I think I 'member Jesus sayin' something 'bout Mr. Bordeaux takin' care of me when you're gone. He said that you wouldn't 'member me but we would always 'member you."

Jaime looked over at Daniel Bordeaux who had noticeably paled at the mention of him taking care of a little girl.

"I'm not going anywhere I'll always be here to take care of you," Jaime said these things with tears in her eyes, hoping she was telling her daughter the truth.

"Mommy, I 'member one more thing Jesus told me to tell you."

"What?"

"He said for you to go down to Harold's this morning an draw a will namin' Mr. Bordeaux my legs goodian. He said something 'bout cutting a day, but I don't know what that means. He said you would know what it meant."

"Are you sure he didn't say to name Mr. Bordeaux your legal guardian, your custodian."

Lavis Ann brightened, "Yeah that's it. What you said."

"Did he say when I was supposed to do all this?"

"He said soon as I waked up I needed to tell you. He said it needed to be done today."

Daniel Bordeaux looked at Jaime Iron with a look of abject horror on his face. "Don't you even think about naming me Lavis's guardian. I don't know anything about raising little girls. Don't you even consider it!"

"Daniel, I consider all direct orders from God. Didn't it sound like an order to you?"

"No, it sounded to me like a little girl had a dream after two traumatic days."

"Is there anything you believe?"

"Ma'am, for years I've been trained to follow procedure. I've found most unexplained things can be explained with patience, perseverance and good police work. I will admit however these cases have a lot of unexplained things, more so than usual. Even though I don't know yet what the answers are I assure you I don't believe you have been visited by angels. I don't believe an angel is the killer. I believe someone is misleading you in order to kill your remaining girl."

"Then how can you explain the cut in your arm? How do you explain your leg? I know you're a smart man, explain these things?"

"I can't explain what I've seen? Nevertheless I don't believe all of these things are supernatural or biblical in nature."

Jaime shook her head in amazement, turned and walked down the hall. Seeing she wasn't going to get through to him, she decided she would get ready and go down to Harold's. "Make yourself a cup of coffee; pot's in the kitchen, cups are in the cabinet above the coffeemaker. Lavis Ann, stay with Mr. Bordeaux until I get out of the shower."

"Are you gonna be my new daddy?

"What…why would you ever come up with the idea I was daddy material?"

"I don' know. I never had a daddy 'fore an I…well…see I figered you would make a good daddy. Jesus tole me in my dream you would. 'Sides Mommy likes you."

"You had a dream honey; dreams aren't real."

"No, it was real."

Daniel looked at the young girl with apprehension. Lavis Ann Iron was entirely convinced her mother was going to leave her to become an angel; of all things. He didn't know where she got the idea he was going to take care of her. Where would she have gotten the idea her mother was going to leave her in the care of an old man? What in the hell did he know about raising little girls. He didn't have a clue what raising a girl would require, he didn't even think he could raise a boy. Surely no one would saddle him with a young child at his age. He was retirement age for Christ's sake. He was old enough to be this kid's grandfather.

"Are we still gonna live here when Mommy's gone. Jesus said you didn't have a house…he said you had a parkment I don' know if I can live in a parkment. You'll have to live here if you take care of me won' you? I gotta have a place to live I can't live in the park like you, can I?"

"I don't live in the park. I live in an apartment, in Birmingham."

"What's a-partment is that like a house? An where's Birmenham is it close to Florence? Or Russellville? I don't think I want to live in Birmenham I'd rather live here. Is it 'kay ifin we jus' live here in my house stead of a partment in Birmenham?"

"Honey, it's perfectly okay if you live here in the house with your mother. I however will continue to live in Birmingham in my apartment without either you or your mother."

"No. No, Jesus tole me you'd take care of me when Mommy was gone. I think she'll be gone in a coupla days. I'm just a little girl; I need someone to take care of me until it's time to lead God's Kids outta the wilderness. Don't you think I'll need someone to take care of me when Mommy's gone?"

Daniel walked into the kitchen found the coffeepot, reached above the coffeepot opened the door and found a cup. Pouring himself a cup of coffee he began to ponder what life would be like with a little girl living with him. It had been years since anyone lived with him for more than twenty four hours. He'd had women stay the night, but he had always made sure they knew perfectly where they stood. He wasn't looking for a wife, nor was he looking for a family, ready-made or otherwise.

"Do you live by yourself down in Birmenham? Or am I gonna get a new Mommy? Do I have a bedroom there?"

"Yes I live by myself, no you're not going to get a new Mommy; no you don't have a bedroom there. I have only one bedroom; I only have one bed, one chair, no place for little girls to live. So I guess I'll have to keep living by myself."

"But…well don't you think I'm gonna need a bedroom?"

"I don't think you are going to get a bedroom at my place. I live by myself. I'm not going to be taking care of you."

"Well who's gonna take care of me?"

"Your Mommy."

"But what if Mommy can't take care of me anymore? Then who's gonna take care of me?"

"I don't know maybe your grandparents, or one of your aunts or uncles or some other relative."

"What's a relative? An why would ants take care of me? Ants don' really take care of people do they?"

"You don't have any aunts?"

"Yeah," Lavis brightened for a moment then said, "we've got ants I fell in the…an ant bed last year an mommy had to come in here and strip me out of my clothes an wipe all the ants offin me. They was bitin' me see an I was screaming an crying. But back then I was a little girl not a big girl like I am now."

"No, not ants like bugs, aunts like…" Daniel paused. "Well they would be either your mother's sisters or your daddy's sisters."

Lavis Ann looked puzzled then said "I didn't know my Mommy had sisters; where's Mommy's sisters at?"

Good Lord talking to a seven year old girl was like talking to some of the bosses he'd had through the years. Lavis Ann seemed to take anything he said and twist it around to fit her understanding of the world. Now he had her believing her mother had sisters. Where did she come up with these ideas? Damn, talking to her was like trying to decipher some weird code. Why was he even trying to carry on a conversation with her? Daniel thought for a moment before deciding he wasn't trying to carry on a conversation with her, he was defending himself from a verbal barrage.

"Mr. Bordeaux?"

"Yes…What do you want now?"

Lavis looked up at him with tears on her face. "I just wanted to ask you a question. Why're you bein' mean to me?"

"I'm not being mean to you."

"You yelled at me."

"I didn't yell at you."

"You did," she said as she stamped her foot for emphasis.

God someone needed to yell at her; she was being a little brat. Children should be seen and not heard. Daniel softened his tone and asked again, "What do you want honey?"

"Never mind, I won't ask if you're goin' to be mean to me. I was just goin' to ask if you liked my Mommy, but I won't ask now."

"Yes I like your Mommy."

"Isn't she pretty, I think she's the prettiest Mommy in the whole world, don't you?"

"Yes I think she's pretty," Daniel said. He was thinking she was more than pretty, she was gorgeous. Pretty didn't cover it. This little girl's mother was probably the most beautiful woman Daniel had ever seen. She had lost a lot in her short time on earth, a husband, and a daughter, yet her well of strength seemed to have no end.

"So, if Mommy doesn't become an angel, do you think you could still be my daddy?"

"*No!*"

"I thought you liked my mommy?"

"I do like your mommy."

"You don't like me?"

This was like fighting a circle saw. There was no way to win; Lavis Ann Iron's perspective completely escaped Daniel Bordeaux. Where did she get all of these questions, how could she possibly come up with the conclusions she did from the answers he gave.

Chapter Eleven

Jaime unbelted the sword and stepped out of her clothes as she walked into the bathroom. She put her clothes into a hamper walked to the tub and turned on the shower. Jaime normally didn't take showers, she took baths, but today she needed to feel the hot water pounding on her tired muscles. When she had the water at the right temperature she stepped into the tub. Immediately the hot—almost too hot—water began to relax her.

Jaime wet her short hair and shampooed it rinsing it out after only a moment. After applying a conditioner she let it set in her hair and soaped up a washcloth and began to wash her body. As she was doing this she made some remarkable discoveries. Daniel wasn't the only one suddenly healed. Jaime looked down at her stomach where a scar should have run along her bikini line slightly below her navel and just above her pelvic bone, the scar was gone. The scar had been from her C-section birth of the twins; it was gone.

Jaime rapidly checked over the rest of her body finding no scars anywhere, the scar on her left arm from the bike accident when she was a kid was gone as were all the rest. Jaime also noticed she didn't have any blemishes anywhere. Jaime was a natural blonde, but she didn't have the clear skin of some natural blondes. Jaime was prone to freckling, if she stayed out in the sun for as much as one hour without a proper sun block she freckled instead of tanning. As such she had never had clear perfect skin. Now however she did.

Jaime quickly rinsed the conditioner out of her hair and stepped out of the tub getting a towel off the rack to her right. As she dried off it seemed she inhabited someone else's body. She hadn't had this body in years. She hadn't had this body since before Connie and Lavis were born. Jaime's butt was a little tighter as was her stomach, her breasts were a little smaller than they had been but now they stood up like they had at twenty-one. She walked over to the mirror and looked at her face. It too seemed tighter; the crow's feet around her eyes had vanished. All in all she looked like she had at twenty-one when she had first met Arnold. Amazing.

Jaime wrapped her head in a towel and picked up the sword, thinking of Lavis Ann. Suddenly she was standing in the kitchen fully nude except for a towel on her head. Jaime gasped as she realized she was standing directly in front of Daniel Bordeaux and Lavis Ann.

Daniel looked her up and down appraising her, nodded appreciatively and promptly turned his back on her. Other than doctors, Daniel was only the second man in her entire life to see her naked and she turned a brilliant shade of crimson before launching herself down the hallway to the bedroom.

As she ran down the hallway she heard Lavis Ann say to Daniel Bordeaux, "See I tole you she was pretty."

When Jaime was firmly ensconced behind a closed bedroom door she smiled wondering who was embarrassed the most, her or Daniel. Had he nodded his appreciation? Did he like the way she looked? Jaime felt Daniel approved of her nude form and the hot flash of embarrassment faded as she wondered exactly how old he was.

Hadn't he said the steel rod in his leg had been there since before her birth? Hadn't he said he'd been in the Marines when it happened during the Vietnam War? If he had been in the Marines in Vietnam, how old would he be? The Vietnam war had ended in what, seventy-something…say seventy-three…if he had been eighteen in seventy-three how old would he be today? At least sixty…could he really be old? No way! He didn't look a day over forty.

Jaime thought for a minute longer before deciding when she had first met him she had thought him to be in his middle forties to early fifties. Before she had cut him she would have thought he was in his middle forties, now however he only looked to be in his late thirties or at most early forties. Could he actually be sixty-something? If so then he was old enough to be her grandfather almost; no, he wasn't old enough to be her grandfather, but he was certainly old enough to be her father.

If he was old enough to be her father why was she so attracted to him?

Chapter Twelve

Jaime lay on the bed for a moment then got up and found a nice looking business outfit she had worn many years ago. The outfit hadn't fit her in seven, almost eight years. Every year she looked at the outfit—one of her favorites—and wondered why she didn't give it or throw it away, it would never fit again anyway.

As she slipped the skirt over her now slim hips she looked into a full length mirror hung on the bathroom door. Jaime liked what she saw, it wasn't she hadn't liked what she saw days or weeks ago, but this was different. Now she once again had the body of a twenty-one year old instead of the body of a thirty-nine year old mother of twins. Everything was tightened up again, the stretch marks gone the crow's feet gone and she felt wonderful. She looked wonderful.

For the first time in more than eight years she put on a pair of high heels. Since the birth of the twins Jaime hadn't worn a business suit or anything *dressy.* Except for church it was yoga pants and tennis shoes, t-shirts and jeans, average everyday attire which screamed *I'm a housewife and I'm not looking for love.*

Since Daniel had now seen her in her altogether, she felt a little conspicuous as she walked back down the hall in one of her sexiest outfits, but then she was sure Daniel had seen naked women before. Jaime didn't have anything any other woman had, did she? Still she wouldn't have walked out into the kitchen naked knowing he was there.

"We going somewhere Mommy?"

"I'm going to go to see an attorney; you're going to stay here with Daniel."

"Oh no you don't. I'm not a damned babysitter."

"Your language Mr. Boudreaux."

"Sorry, about the language," he said reddening slightly. "But the answer is no, if you leave so am I. The girl goes with us."

"No. The Angel Michael was very specific. Lavis is not to leave the property. Here she is protected until I have the chance to kill the Angel of Death."

"What do you know about killing? I bet you have never killed anything more significant than a cockroach."

"Nevertheless I have been chosen to be the one who ends the Angel of Death's reign. If I must kill Azrael to protect Lavis Ann, kill her I will."

"Somehow I believe you have the physical ability, but I don't know if you have the mental fortitude."

"We'll see, but in the meantime, you will certainly stay here and watch Lavis won't you? Please I'll only be gone for an hour or two at the most." Jaime looked at her watch it was almost noon. "I'll be back by no later than two-thirty. Please. Okay then I'll see you in a couple of hours." Jaime kissed him on the cheek on her way out of the door, feeling a slight tingle as she did.

Daniel watched her close the door wondering all the while why he was going along with this. He knew she was playing him, using her charms to get her way, but not knowing exactly how to keep her from doing it. He watched her walk out to her Jeep Grand Cherokee. Daniel followed her form as she sat down in the white Jeep, wishing one day he would be able to have a woman like her—knowing all the while he never would. Jaime Iron was a lady, and he was an old tired state cop. Jaime was too good for him, but a man could dream couldn't he?

"I tole you Mommy likes you."

"Whatever gave you that idea?"

"She kissed you didn't she? I never seen her kiss anyone 'cept me an Connie an I know she likes us."

"Just because she kissed me doesn't mean she likes me."

"I think you're gonna be my new daddy. I hope so; I don't remember my real daddy. A little girl needs a daddy."

"Once again, I'm not going to be your daddy, I'm too old for your mother."

"She doesn't think so. We'll see, I bet you're gonna be my new daddy. I think I'll start calling you Daddy now…That'll be ok won't it."

"It certainly will not. I'm not gonna…I'm not going," damn he was starting to talk like her. "No you can't call me daddy. I'm not your daddy, and I'm not going to be your daddy."

"Mommy tole me one time some men play games, are you foolin' me?"

Daniel saw after only ten minute this was going to be the hardest two hours of his life. He decided after twenty minutes he would rather be in the jungle as the VC charged the wire. Suddenly he had an idea. "Do you watch TV? There is a TV here isn't there?"

"Sure, I watch TV."

"Think you could watch TV while I make some calls."

"Do you need to use the phone? Come on I'll show you where it is." Lavis Ann took his hand and led him over to the couch. "Sit right there," she said.

Daniel looked around, but didn't see a phone. "I thought you said you would show me the phone."

"I am silly…you sit right there and don't move an I'll be right back. Promise me you won't move?"

"I promise."

He sat there as she rushed down the hall and in to the bedroom Jaime had come out of. Only a moment later, she came back out at a breakneck speed holding a white cordless phone. "Here you go. I'll sit right over there," she motioned at what Daniel thought must be an entertainment center. I'll turn on the TV, but I'll turn it on real quiet so you can hear who you're talkin' to on the phone. 'Kay?"

"Okay."

Lavis went over to the entertainment center and opened the doors on it revealing a large color television. The doors were slid back into the entertainment center and another door was opened to reveal an ancient VCR. It had been years since Bordeaux had seen a working VCR. Lavis opened a door below the television and after much thought decided on a tape to put into the VCR.

Soon a purple dinosaur filled the screen singing about loving everyone. Daniel tried not to be interested in what Lavis was doing, but he found it intriguing she could sit and watch this garbage and not say a word.

Daniel picked up the phone and placed the first of the many phone calls he had to make. The first call went to his boss, who advised him nothing new was happening on the case, and after a heated discussion agreed to leave Daniel on protection detail until further notice. After several more phone calls he had all of his business taken care of, and everyone knew where he was.

Daniel had nothing better to do than watch Lavis Ann Iron—literally. Lavis sat in front of the television singing softly under her breath the words to each song. As she sang, Daniel found himself getting a little sleepy. There was no real reason for him to be sleepy, he had slept more in the past few days than he normally did, but nevertheless he was sleepy. Daniel looked at his watch wondering how long Jaime had been gone and was astonished to find she had only been gone for twenty-five minutes. It would still be several hours before she returned.

With a smile on his face—remembering the brief kiss—Daniel drifted off to sleep.

Chapter Thirteen

Jaime pulled out of the driveway smiling slightly. She couldn't believe she had the impudence to kiss the gruff old policeman. Kiss him she had though; she wasn't the least bit sorry she had, even if it was a peck on the cheek. Daniel seeing her naked bothered Jaime; but it couldn't be helped now and she wondered if she should have given him even a small kiss so soon. Jaime didn't want Daniel thinking she was a loose woman; she wasn't an impulsive person normally and really didn't know why she'd had the impulse to kiss the man lightly on the cheek.

Jaime usually didn't do anything without considering all of the pros and cons associated with the action. Jaime couldn't afford to do such things. She'd never been afforded the chance to be a child and Jaime was intent on making sure her daughters, well daughter now, had the chance to be a child. No child should have to grow up at ten.

Jaime had been twelve years old when her father had passed away. He'd been sick for a long time prior to his death, but had kept on working at the mill despite his growing fatigue. Jaime had known for six months before her father died he wasn't going to make it. Increasingly he had come in so tired he could do nothing but lay on the couch. Only a few days after Jaime's twelfth birthday, her father had passed quietly in the night.

Jaime found out years later he had been suffering from lung cancer and hadn't wanted her to know.

At ten years old Jaime White had been sentenced to a life of hardship. Jaime lived in no less than eight foster homes in the first two years after her father's death. Each time she left one foster home she hoped against all odds the next home would truly be the family she had been waiting on. For the most part though all the foster families were doing were collecting a check and getting a servant.

Most of the families in the foster care system were decent people, to their own children anyway, but she wasn't one of theirs. So Jaime ended up most of the time feeling like Cinderella, forced into kitchen scullery while the other children her age in the house—if there were any—were treated like young princes and princesses. After a while Jaime began to develop an attitude and sooner or later she would be moved to another foster home.

By the time Jaime was fourteen, Jaime had given up all hope she would be adopted by any of the families. Turning fourteen brought on a new set of problems. Several months before Jaime's fourteenth birthday she had her first menstrual cycle. Following her first menstrual cycle things began to happen to her young body.

While Jaime had always been a pretty young girl, she had been as thin as a rail and as straight up and down as a bamboo shoot. However after her first menstrual cycle her body began to change, first Jaime's breasts began to grow, soon thereafter she began to develop hips and a more woman-like figure. While this normally wouldn't have presented any problems in a normal teenager's life. In Jaime's world it was a huge problem. Jaime was living in people's homes and she wasn't in any way related to them. There was the problem with teenage boys for one thing, but it was a normal part of life and she could deal with boys. The problem she couldn't deal with was the men of the house. More than one of her so-called foster fathers had climbed into her bed after the lights were out expecting sex.

The first time it had happened, she had screamed bloody murder waking up everyone in the house. Everyone had come rushing into her room expecting anything except what they found, Daddy with his pajamas around his ankles and a hysterical girl. Jaime would never forget the first time it had happened. The man's name had been David Dodge.

Mr. Dodge was supposedly a pillar of the community. He was the local bank president, deacon in the church and all the usual stuff associated with a man of his stature in the community. Yet this seemingly wonderful man had climbed into her bed at one in the morning, with a hard-on and groping hands. Jaime had woken the minute he had climbed into bed with her and while she didn't exactly know his intent, she knew it wasn't good. When David Dodge had torn her panties off with rough hands and pulled her thin t-shirt over her head, she knew whatever he was doing wasn't right. So she had screamed, and despite the man's protests and warnings she had screamed and screamed until the entire household was standing in her room with the light on and looking at her standing naked and David Dodge on the other side of the bedroom his hard-on diminishing rapidly.

Mrs. Dodge walked in the room to see what was happening. She looked at her husband, his member now soft and flaccid and gave him a look that would have instantly turned steam into ice. After staring at him a moment, her face red with rage, Mrs. Dodge turned her glare on Jaime.

"Well you little whore, I give you a place to live, put a roof over your head and this is how you repay me?" she had asked. Jaime tried to protest, saying she hadn't done anything, but the lady of the house was having none of it. "You little slut, what do you think you're doing? Do you think your little twat could handle my man? Did you think you could screw your way into this family? Get out; get out of my house now."

"Mrs. Dodge I didn't do anything. Mr. Dodge, he came into…"

"I don't want to hear your pack of lies, they've been told before. You're not the first little girl to come here and try what you tried. You get out of my house now. Get your things and get out."

"But where am I going to go?"

"You little whore; you should have considered where you were going to live before you tried taking my place."

After several more failed foster home placements, Jaime ended up in a state facility. While the state home didn't have the finest accommodations, she was safe, and no one molested her. Jaime remained until few days after her eighteenth birthday, and she'd been on her own since.

Jaime knew she didn't have anyone to depend on, so she managed to finish College with a bachelor's degree in banking and finance only two and one-half years after she entered. Jaime then had moved to Huntsville and after only a few days she had found a job with a small finance company.

Jaime worked for the finance company for almost a year seeing the backstabbing and corporate greed going on there before she decided she didn't want to be in the banking world. Jaime had seen the light however; she now knew where her place would be. Jaime had taken a few night classes and in six months had her real-estate license. Two days after receiving her license she had hired on with Roger's firm and began her real estate career.

In her first years, she had exceeded everyone's expectations by a wide margin. Roger was extremely proud of the fact he had hired this hungry young woman. Jaime White was a broker's dream come true. Jaime did whatever it took to sell a property short of lying. She wouldn't lie for anyone or anything. As a result, her integrity soon became the talk of the town and their business increased exponentially. Jaime was a salesperson through and through, but she had heart of a teacher. Many times she ended up talking the person out of a property they couldn't afford and steering them to a property they could afford, or a property better suited to their investment strategy.

Roger had been very angry the first time she had talked a person out of a property until the referrals started to come in. Soon his agency was known as the little agency with the big heart and Jaime was the top salesperson in the northern part of Alabama. Rogers Real Estate quickly became the top producer in Huntsville. Soon he let Jaime do as she pleased; she wasn't doing anything unethical, so he let her go.

After working for Roger for ten years, Jaime had met a slightly older man named Arnold Iron. Arnold worked for a regional branch of a large financial institution. Jaime immediately liked the older man (he was 46 to her 29) and agreed to accompany him to dinner when he had asked. From there it was as they say history. Only ten months from the time of the initial date Arnold Iron asked Jaime White to marry him. One year to the day from their first date, Jaime became Mrs. Arnold Iron.

Chapter Fourteen

Ben McElroy stood looking at the meager evidence. The press had begun to call the victims sacrificial lambs, and the killer the Angel of Darkness. Where had the press gotten the details of the killings? Well never mind where they had gotten the details, there was one sick puppy on the loose and Ben intended to be one of the ones who brought the Angel of Darkness to justice. Friggin press calling these kids the sacrificial lambs, at least they hadn't found out about the pictures or they would be calling him the Photographer or some BS.

Ben examined the last photograph received by the Iron woman. It was different, so different as to seem supernatural. The girls frolicked in the warm sunshine, playing on a beach on one of the area lakes. They seemed oblivious to the danger within their sight. Only three days ago Jaime Iron had received this picture and one of her children was dead.

There was something significant in this picture. There had to be, didn't there? After Ben stared at the picture for more than an hour, his eyes were beginning to get blurry. Then Ben saw something neither he, nor anyone else had seen before. The woman in the picture wasn't Jaime Iron. The woman resembled Jaime slightly, but it wasn't her. Who was the woman?

Ben wondered if the other mothers bore a resemblance to Jaime. The Bureau and other police agencies had focused on the little girls. Did the mothers resemble one another? Ben removed the files one by one seeing for the first time the mothers of the sacrificed lambs. One by one he realized they, while not looking exactly alike, bore a striking resemblance to one another.

Ben looked again at the moving picture in his hand. It was definitely not Jaime Iron, but the resemblance was uncanny. As Ben looked at the picture the blonde woman on the beach turned and looked directly out of the picture at Ben. Her hair changed from straight blonde to a deep dark curly ebony. She walked to the edge of the picture and stared directly at Ben. *I'm coming for you,* she seemed to say.

Ben shook his head to clear the cobwebs. He had stared at the photograph so long he was hallucinating. For a minute he'd believed the woman's hair changed colors and she was looking at him. There was no doubt though, the woman in the picture was not Jaime Iron. Could it be the woman in the picture was the killer? Or could she possibly be an accomplice? Quickly he picked up the picture of the Jarnigan girl. It was a scene not unlike the scene with the Iron girls, but once again the woman in the picture was not Mrs. Jarnigan. Who…could it be? He held the pictures close together and there was no doubt; the woman frolicking on the beach in the Iron picture and the woman hiking in the woods in the Jarnigan picture were the same woman. This was something. This was something he needed to talk to Daniel about.

Ben removed his cell-phone from his belt and pushed the one-touch button to dial Daniel's phone. While Ben was waiting for the cell-phones to connect he wondered why Daniel was still on protection detail. There were so many other officers who would have jumped at the chance for overtime pay, and the state needed Daniel Boudreaux's expertise in solving this crime. What the hell was the boss thinking?

The cell-phones didn't link up. Ben got Daniel's voice mail and left a message, he needed Daniel to call him immediately. After leaving the message on Daniel's phone, Ben called the captain.

"Captain Gaines."

"Captain, this is Ben. I think I've found something significant in the Sacrificial Lambs case."

"What have you found?"

"I think this is something you need to see. It may break the case, it may not"

"So tell me what you've got."

"I really think you need to see this, have you got a few moments?"

"Yeah, sure bring it on up."

Ben picked up the photos of all of the girls and walked down the hall in the direction of the captain's office. As Ben walked he flipped through the pictures one by one and in every picture the woman was the same. How could no one have noticed the lady in the pictures was not the parent?

"Then the FBI's profile is wrong, or the killer is working with a partner."

"That's what I would think. I think the woman is the killer, not an accomplice."

Captain Gaines held the pictures up one by one and looked at the woman in each of the pictures. The lady was stunning, an angel if there ever was one. She didn't look capable of harming a child, but then Captain Gaines had been in law enforcement long enough to understand not everything was as it appeared. Sometimes even beautiful people were so damaged the human psyche could appear to be one thing when there was truly a monster underneath a facade of friendliness and pleasing personality.

"Get some copies of these pictures made and put it out to all the enforcement agencies. This woman shouldn't be too hard to find. I want her picture on the evening news. By this time tomorrow I want everyone in the tristate area to know what she looks like. We should begin getting calls by the end of the newscast."

"Yes sir...Sir, may I ask a question?"

"Yeah, what?"

"I know you've been in this business a lot longer than I have. I...Why would a woman do something like this? I don't understand."

"Son, I've been trying to figure out the same thing for more than forty years. You know Daniel and I were partners years ago; I had been a Detective for a year when Daniel came home from the war in Vietnam. Then as now he was a hard cynical man, and he had seen more than his share of death, I suspect he had inflicted more than his share of death. Because of his determination we rose rapidly through the ranks and the two of us made lieutenant in less than ten years. Along the way we managed to solve murder case after murder case. Some were simple straightforward man kills other man over a woman, or man kills woman after catching her in a moment of passion with someone other than himself. Those cases are relatively easy to understand. Most of those people if they had it to do over again would take it back. I've seen a hundred murderers break down and cry over what they perceive to be their loss."

"Everyone has been so angry at times one little slip would have ended someone else's life, but this is not what this case is about. I've also seen drunks and drug-addicts kill, but being an addict doesn't necessarily make you a bad person, they were poor-spirited people with a problem they couldn't control and weren't thinking rationally at the time."

"This is different. This is a cold-blooded killer. This killer is with pre-meditation going about the pre-planned execution of a group of little girls. This I don't understand. My only thought is this person is crazy. If it is the woman in the pictures she's either crazy or…and I hesitate to say this…but she's an evil sociopath. There are some people out there who don't fit the mold of gentle society. These people are not crazy. They go about what would seem to be normal lives all the while planning heinous acts. When these people are caught, and most are eventually they know exactly what they have done and show no remorse for these acts. So I can honestly say I believe either this person is sincerely disturbed or is completely and entirely evil. Does this answer your question?"

"Well no not exactly. But I do see where you're coming from."

"I don't know how to answer it any other way."

"Why if I may be so bold as to ask are you leaving one of your best investigators on protection detail?" Ben thought for a moment then said "I didn't know you and Daniel were partners."

Captain Gaines leaned back in his chair smiling as he remembered. "Daniel was the best partner I ever had. When he became Captain of the Homicide Division . . ."

"Daniel was a Captain?"

"Daniel was the Captain. Well for almost one whole month anyway."

"I never knew he was Captain."

"He was promoted to Captain after only ten years on the force. After only fifteen days, he decided being the boss wasn't what he wanted. See Daniel is a soldier. He couldn't stand being the one in the office making the decisions; he wanted to be out on the front lines catching the killers. Then as now it wasn't possible. It took him fifteen days to resign this position, while making sure I got the position. He stepped aside and made sure I was promoted into a position which was rightfully his. As a condition of my promotion, he made me promise I would allow him free rein on his cases. Since then he has never gave me a reason to go back on my promise. Daniel's record is exemplary. Daniel has solved every single murder case I have assigned him to. This has been the most trying case of Daniel's career. Six years spent looking for one killer, and he tells me now he's on the cusp of solving it…so I'm inclined to give him free rein. I don't know why he insists on remaining as the protector of the Iron woman, but I know Daniel. If he thinks it is necessary to remain where he is there is a good reason."

Chapter Fifteen

Jaime turned on her right turn signal and pulled into the parking place in front of Harold's office. Harold was and had been the family attorney since Jaime and Arnold married. Harold had been a family friend for more years than she cared to count now.

"Good Afternoon Jennifer," Jaime said as she walked into the office. "Is Harold in?"

"No hon he's not here right now. Harold left for lunch almost an hour ago. He should be back any minute though. Do you need to see him, or did you stop by to chat?"

"I need to see him."

"What about?"

"Some personal business."

"You might as well tell me about it now honey. You know I am the one who types up all of this stuff anyway."

"I need to change my will."

"I see, and the reason for this?"

"Let's say I had a dream."

Who would you like to be the new beneficiary?"

"Actually I would like to change more than the beneficiaries. I need to change the person who has guardianship of my remaining girl."

"Why the sudden change? And who is this new guardian?"

"I'd rather not discuss the reasons behind the change, but Lavis Ann's new guardian will be Daniel Bordeaux of Birmingham."

"The detective?"

"Yeah."

"Honey you're not being pressured in some way are you? I mean . . . well I think it's highly unusual for you to want to change this only a few days after you lost Connie. Isn't this something which could wait for a few months?"

"No it can't wait. I want to leave all my personal belongings in a trust for Lavis, with Daniel as the trustee. I need Harold to set it up today. I have a feeling I won't live to the end of the week. I will be back to sign the papers tomorrow. I guess what I am saying is; I don't really need to see Harold; I need him to do this will for me. Can he have all the papers ready by tomorrow?"

"Certainly, if you think it's necessary. But I think you are overreacting. I don't know what to think about your belief you won't live through the end of the week."

"I know this sounds crazy, but you have to believe me. There are things going on I couldn't possibly explain, please promise me you'll take care of this."

"Okay, I'll take care of it. But I don't have to agree with it."

"Thanks Jennifer. You're a lifesaver."

Azrael stood looking at the home where the policeman and the young girl were holed up. She knew God's protection was absolute, but she couldn't understand why God was letting the Archangel Michael protect the young girl. Why would God extend his protection to this one little girl? Azrael knew God loved the little children. It was one of the reasons Azrael had chosen the little girls. Each one of them represented an exceptional version of the best of everything God had created. They were so innocent, and so trusting. Why couldn't children stay young and innocent? Children did not doubt for an instant the existence of God if they had been taught anything about *Him*.

As for the Iron woman, Azrael would take care of her sooner or later. Angel's sword or not, Jaime Iron was no match for the *Supreme Angel of Death*. Azrael would keep her word. This very evening everyone within one mile of Jaime's home would die. Azrael would wait until the woman returned home, and then the destruction would begin.

Nine miles away Jaime Iron walked out of the attorney's office and felt a chill. It was as if someone was thinking terrible thoughts about her. Jaime reached out with her mind in a way she hadn't known had existed only yesterday and connected with the mind of the angel Azrael. Jaime felt the chill of the angel's anger. Azrael was pissed at Jaime for wounding her.

Jaime shook off the chill and walked down the street to the insurance office. Jaime stood for only a moment in Sharon Tate's waiting room before she was admitted to see her insurance agent.

"Baby, I'm so sorry about Connie, I wish there were something else I could...I'm sorry Jaime. I have the check, you may need it to bury her with." Seeing the tears on Jaime's face, Sharon wished she'd been more tactful. A hundred thousand dollar check wasn't going to replace this lady's little girl. Sharon stood up and walked around her desk and hugged Jaime. "I'm sorry Jaime."

Jaime wiped the tears from her eyes and tried to think through this logically. She came to Sharon's office with a purpose, and getting a check to bury Connie with had not even been in her thoughts. Jaime Iron had come to the insurance office to make sure her remaining daughter was taken care of. "Well I hope this won't take long, but I need to change the beneficiary on my insurance policy. I would also like to add an additional five hundred thousand to my policy. Is it possible today?"

"Well it's a little unusual for a housewife to have a million dollars in life insurance, but I don't think it will be a problem. We'll run it through…You…uh you're not…you're not planning on dying next week are you? I mean, well I…you don't have something medically wrong with you do you? No cancer or anything? If you've been recently been diagnosed with something life threatening I couldn't write the policy…and if you commit suicide…well the policy doesn't pay."

No…nothing like that. I…well I feel like I need this. I mean if something were to happen to me what would Lavis Ann do? I don't want her to have to…well I don't want her to have to go through what I did."

"Jaime, with a million dollars in life insurance money and a good guardian, Lavis will never want for anything. Who did you have in mind for the life insurance beneficiary?

"Well, the beneficiary should be Daniel Bordeaux, he's from Birmingham."

"Daniel Bordeaux, isn't he the detective, the one investigating the murders?"

"He is."

"Why him if I may ask."

"I hate to be blunt with you Sharon, but really it's none of your business."

"You're right, I'm sorry."

"Sharon...I'm sorry, I didn't mean to snap at you, but..."

"No, you were right it is none of my business; don't think a thing of it. I know it's been a rough time for you these past few days. If I lost one of my babies...I'd be a little testy."

When Jaime walked out of Sharon's office she held the insurance check for Connie, wishing she had something a little more substantial to hold on to than a piece of paper. Jaime started to cry, and for the first time since Azrael had taken Connie Kay, Jaime broke down and cried.

Jaime hadn't really noticed she was lying on the sidewalk in tears when she felt a hand shaking her. Jaime looked up into the caring eyes of a very large man wearing the brown uniform of the Sheriff's dept.

"You okay ma'am?" Eric Sandusky asked Jaime.

"Uh...sure Sheriff...it's just..."

Eric looked down at the woman knowing instantly who she was. This was the Iron woman, what was her name? Wasn't she the woman Daniel Bordeaux was protecting right now? What in the hell was she doing lying on the sidewalk in front of Lori's office?

"Mrs. Iron are you okay?"

"Yeah, I…just…"

"Here come with me; I'll have Lori make you a cup of coffee." Sheriff Sandusky scooped up Jaime in his arms as if she were a small child, carrying her the few yards into a real estate office right beside Sharon Tate's office. "Lori, can you get this lady a cup of coffee or tea?"

"Sure, is something wrong?"

"Lori, this is Jaime Iron, and she…well she broke down out on the sidewalk. I thought…well maybe we need to help her out a little. She's had a bad couple of days."

"Sweetie, would you like coffee, sweet tea, or maybe a soft drink, or a bottle of water?"

"No…I'm fine…I just…" Jaime started sobbing again uncontrollably. Lori felt this woman's need for affection. Lori could see right now what Jaime Iron really needed was a friend, not a beverage. Lori walked over to Jaime and took her into her arms pressing her tear-stained face into her shoulder. "I'm sorry baby I know I don't really know you but if you need anything, anything at all you lean on me. Eric and I can't have kids. We've adopted three children, and I couldn't bear the thoughts of losing even one of them. I don't know how you're dealing with this."

"Thanks…Lori I really appreciate this, but I need to go. I need to go back home, I had some business I really needed to take care of before…well I needed to take care of some business."

"Sure you wouldn't like a coffee? I'll be more than happy to put on a pot of coffee. I'm sure Eric would like a cup anyway."

"Sure, honey put on a pot of coffee. I need a cup, and I wouldn't feel comfortable letting Mrs. Iron leave until she has her emotions under control. I may need to drive her home."

Looking at Jaime Iron, Lori felt a tinge of jealousy at the thought of Eric driving this woman anywhere, but jealousy came from her old way of thinking. Eric was a good man. In the years since Eric and Lori married, Lori never had one instant to doubt Eric. Why was she even thinking this?

Jaime sat on a comfortable couch in Lori's office kitchen, her tears ruining her makeup while Lori efficiently made a pot of coffee. When the coffee was finished brewing Lori removed two cups from a cabinet and poured the steaming liquid into them. "Do you take cream or sugar?"

"Both, I'll do it." Jaime stood and tried to collect her wits and walked over to the kitchen counter. Lori placed two containers on the counter beside Jaime's cup and stepped back out of the way. Jaime noticed she had something clenched in her fist. She opened her hand and saw it was the insurance check. This brought on a new flood of tears.

Eric watched the young lady with a mourning heart. While Eric couldn't imagine losing his and Lori's son, he could identify with her pain. Eric, like almost everyone on the planet had lost someone he loved once.

Jaime wadded up the check and tossed it into the garbage can located at the end of the counter. She didn't want this money. She didn't want money. Jaime wanted her little girl back. Why had the *Angel* bitch taken her little girl?

Unconsciously Jaime touched the hilt of the sword while thinking of Azrael. Immediately Jaime was transported to Azrael's location. Suddenly Jaime was looking at the Angel's back as Azrael looked at the Iron home.

Eric and Lori were stunned. Jaime Iron vanished before their eyes. "Eric? What happened?"

"I don't know hon, she vanished." Eric walked over to the trash can and picked up the wadded up ball Jaime had thrown into the trash can. When Eric unfolded the piece of paper and saw it was a check. It didn't take a state detective to understand why Jaime Iron was crying. Eric showed the check to Lori and almost immediately there was a hint of moisture in her eyes.

"Can you carry the check down to the bank and deposit it for her? At least she won't have to see it again."

"Sure . . . well I could if I knew what bank she used."

"Well you're the sheriff, if you can't find out what bank Jaime Iron uses for her checking account, I'm voting for someone else next time you run for office. Find out and deposit it for her. Call Peter if you have to. If you can't find out, I'll assure you Peter can. Hell he practically owns the world."

Eric walked out of Sandusky Real Estate, and looked to the north. Clouds were building rapidly over Littleville.

Chapter Sixteen

Jaime drew the sword soundlessly and with a swift sure stroke she swung the sword at the angel's neck, intending to remove her head with the single stroke. At the last moment, as if Azrael felt the air currents moving before the sword she moved to the side and Jaime's sword sliced through nothing but thin air.

"So once again you have tried to kill me," Azrael said as she turned around to face Jaime. "Didn't you learn from the last exchange killing an angel isn't as easy as taking a human life? By all the power God has vested in me, I could now take your life as easily as you turn off a light switch. The people of this town will pay for your insubordination. The people of Colbert Heights better have their lives square with the Heavenly Father, for they will meet him within the hour."

Jaime looked up into the face of the Archangel and saw an entity on the edge of lunacy. Jaime had never really seen crazy until now. Azrael wasn't evil, she was on the razors-edge of insanity. Like a sad clown, Azrael smiled at Jaime and began to spin.

Jaime saw clouds boil in over the horizon. Huge ink black clouds piled up against the horizon, blocking out the sun. All around the spinning angel leaves were beginning to tear away from the trees, while the winds picked up. Jaime ran for the house watching as the angel spun faster and faster until a funnel cloud reached the heavens. The wind picked up as the sky darkened. Day turned into the darkest night. Rain began to pour out of the black cumulous clouds. Rain fell in sheets as the sky became as dark as a cave. Jaime, still holding the angel's sword suddenly wished she were in her house. Her wish became reality as she was looking out of her picture window into her manicured yard. As Jaime looked out of her window she noticed something she hadn't noticed. It would seem her property was inside an invisible fence. Directly above her home the sun shined as if there was no weather pattern raging outside.

"What in the hell is going on out there?" Daniel asked.

"Azrael is destroying the town," Jaime said matter-of-factly.

"What are…you…What. Are. You. Talking about? What do you mean destroying the town?"

"Remember this morning when I told you Azrael said she would kill everyone in this town for my insubordination?"

"Yeah, I remember you saying something about…"

"Well it's happening."

"What's happening?" You don't think? No this is just a storm."

"Let's go outside."

"What are you kidding?"

"Lavis Ann, where are you? Come out here and I'll show you a demonstration of God's power."

"You're not seriously going to try to make this child believe this is supernatural, are you?"

"And why wouldn't I? I know you can hear the storm, but have you seen it?"

"Mommy, you're home! I din't think you'd be home this soon. I din't hear you drive up, how'd you get home?"

"Never mind honey, come on I'll show you something unbelievable. Lavis?"

"What mommy?"

"You know where our property lines are don't you?"

"Property lines?" Lavis Ann looked confused.

"You know where our yard ends and Mr. Bristow's yard starts don't you?"

Lavis Ann's face lit up with understanding. "Yeah mommy I know where our yard is."

"Okay sweetie, but you have to stay in our yard, don't go...don't cross over into Mr. Bristow's yard. Okay sweetie?"

"Okay Mommy."

Jaime took Lavis by the hand and walked out into the yard. Brilliant sunshine lit up her yard, but around her property lines the scene was entirely different. Jaime watched as Azrael dropped out of the funnel cloud and it disappeared. In Mr. Bristow's yard Azrael stood watching the trio.

"Daniel, there she is. There is the angel Azrael."

Daniel looked at a beautiful dark haired woman in a long flowing robe of the whitest silk. He reached behind his belt, walking toward the darkness enveloping the surrounding landscape with the exception of Jaime's property. "No Daniel, don't." Jaime shouted as he continued toward the exotic dark haired beauty. When he was within twenty feet of her, Azrael began to spin again as if she were on an axis right at her feet.

Faster and faster she spun until a funnel cloud reached into the black clouds above her. Daniel watched as the grass, trees and bushes pulled from the ground became one with the wind. Mr. Bristow's house blew apart as if it had been in the direct path of a nuclear warhead. The trees and bushes were tossed around in circles as the funnel cloud became larger and larger until finally Daniel couldn't really see the sides anymore, he could only see what seemed to be a slowly moving mass of flying debris. He couldn't see the trees anymore, nor could he see the flying bricks or the mass of electrical wire once contained inside the walls of Mr. Bristow's home. Faster and faster they spun, each large item became a thousand smaller items. Chairs became splinters; splinters became dust particles.

Slowly, ever so slowly the funnel moved away from Jaime's property. In forty five minutes the funnel cloud had only moved one hundred yards, but the damage path was unmistakable. Where the funnel cloud touched, nothing remained, buildings, grass, trees, all disappeared. Nothing remained, it was barren as the face of the moon. The trio standing in the protected yard could hear the wind howling. This was not any ordinary storm. This was the storm of the century.

Ahead of the funnel cloud, it rained and hailstones as large as basketballs fell from the sky. The hail beat buildings and trees into splinters the splinters were picked up by the winds and cast about until they were no more. In horror, the trio watched as people tried to run from the storm only to be beaten to a pulp by the basketball sized hail then ripped limb from limb by the wind and the debris it carried. They watched as storm houses were pulled from the ground –as if a large gardener were pulling weeds from his garden— then ground into dust which became a thin slurry. People inside houses were hurled screaming into the wind never to be seen or heard from ever again.

With a look of abject horror on her young face, Lavis watched the gruesome sight. "Mommy, can we go back into the house? I don't think I want to see any more of this."

"I don't think I want to see any more of this either, come on." Jaime took Lavis by the hand and led her into the house as Daniel continued to stand in the yard and watch with a morbid fascination.

Daniel had never seen anything as devastating as this was. This was much worse than anything he had ever seen in the war. Daniel had seen buildings blown into splinters, but after the bomb blast there was always bricks and lumber—mostly damaged or broken – but recognizable as former building materials. Here there was nothing recognizable. Following even a nuclear blast, there would be items damaged but intact. Not here, here only a flat deep layer of enriched soil remained. Only a soggy mess of what would soon be the richest farm land in the world remained.

Daniel sat on the ground and for the first time in his adult life prayed to a God only moments ago he had doubted the existence of. Until he had witnessed this spectacle, Daniel would have doubted the sanity of anyone who believed this was possible. Daniel had doubted the sanity of Jaime Iron, not anymore. Now he believed not only was there a God, but some of God's creations were much more intelligent, powerful and vindictive than even humans were.

Daniel, when he had finished his prayer wondered how he would explain this to the Captain. He had been a witness to an unbelievable event. The press would go wild and he would be expected to recant this experience not only in a report but to the reporters as well. What would he say? What would the report be? Surely he couldn't really write a report telling the truth, could he? He would be laughed out of the Bureau. Suddenly he knew what he would write. Daniel knew what he would tell. Daniel would tell the truth about what he had seen. Nobody would believe it, but who cared what they believed. They wouldn't believe anything anyone said anyway, so why not tell the truth. Why not tell the unbelievers exactly what had happened here? It would be the end of his career as a police officer, but what the hell; he hadn't needed the income from his job for many years now. His investments alone paid more than twenty times his salary each year. After a moments introspection; Daniel Bordeaux decided today would be his last day as an officer of the law. Today Daniel Bordeaux would retire after forty years on the force.

Daniel wondered what he would do with his time. If what Jaime had said was true, he may end up being the guardian of the young girl. He didn't know anything about raising a young girl, but he guessed he would have to learn.

Chapter Seventeen

"Okay, so now I believe you, what do we do now?"

"We do as I said, we protect Lavis."

"And how do we do protect her from a being which can destroy a whole town and make it look like a tornado?"

"She's not to leave this property until the angel Azrael is dead."

"It may not be quite so simple. You yourself said the Archangel Michael's protection wasn't absolute. You yourself said it was for a short time. We might have to hunt this angel down. We will probably have to use the sword to find the angel. Didn't you say the sword transported you to wherever or whomever I

"Yes, it seems if I grasp the handle of the sword and think of a place or person, I am immediately transported to their location."

"Let's see you try it. Grasp the handle of the sword and think of someplace, maybe the kitchen."

Jaime took the handle of the sword and thought of the kitchen. Nothing happened. She concentrated on the area in front of the stove. Nothing happened. "I don't know what…why nothing's happening."

"Are you doing anything different than you generally have done when you were transported? What's different?"

Jaime thought for a moment and couldn't think of anything she was doing different. It took a moment before she realized what she was doing wrong. Jaime had always been thinking of a person before when she had been transported. "Daniel, walk into the kitchen. I think I know what is wrong."

Daniel walked into the kitchen and stood by the stove. Jaime stood in the living room and thought of Daniel, grasping the hilt of the sword as she did. Before she finished the thought completely she was standing before him.

"So now we know as much as we can about the transport mechanism of the sword. You have to be thinking about someone in particular."

"Yeah, Michael said if Azrael took the little girl, all I had to do was grasp the hilt of the sword and I would be transported to her location. I guess this works with others as well."

"Think of someone. Think of someone you know and grasp the handle of the sword. Let's see if you are transported to their location."

Jaime thought of Lori Sandusky sitting in her office in Russellville. When she grasped the handle of her sword, suddenly she was looking at the beautiful young real estate broker. Lori was in what had to be a basement of an expensive home. Beside Lori was an exotic looking lady, what had to be the lady's husband—a large extremely well dressed man—

Sheriff Sandusky and three children. The four adults looked at Jaime with an air of confusion as Jaime once again touched the handle of the sword and thought of Lavis Ann. Immediately she was with her young girl again.

"Did you see who you were thinking of?"

"Yeah."

"What else does the sword do? It seems to have other magical powers. Well they wouldn't be magical; they would be gifts from god."

Jaime thought for a moment before saying, "I noticed I feel and look younger than I did only yesterday. Now I have the body of a twenty-one year old instead of the body I had only two weeks ago. Do you think this sword has the power to heal injuries and make bodies perfect again?"

"I don't know. Do you want to try it?"

"Sure, on whom?"

"Well we started with me earlier. Do what you did when the steel rod pushed out of my leg."

Jaime pulled the sword from its sheath and held it tightly in her hand. With her other hand, Jaime reached out and touched Daniel's arm and willed herself to feel his pain, to mend his pain.

Daniel felt an out pouring of compassion from the young woman. He felt his spine straighten slightly.

139

He felt his posture return to what it had been thirty years ago. In his mouth suddenly it felt as if he had a mouth full of gravel. Cupping his hand over his mouth he spit the gravel into his palm then looked down at what had to be the fillings out of his teeth. The only thing which seemed to get worse was his vision. His vision went from pretty good to really bad. Daniel couldn't figure this out until he realized he had his contacts in. With the hand not holding the fillings, he removed one of his contacts and was rewarded with perfect vision.

Jaime felt the flood of compassion pouring out of her. She felt his healing process, not as he did but in a different way that she couldn't describe. Before her very eyes, Daniel Bordeaux became the person he had been forty-eight years ago, physically if not emotionally. Jaime watched as his posture straightened, his receding hair line repopulated itself with hair. Jaime watched him become leaner, more muscular. She watched his nose—it had to have been broken at one time—straighten itself and the various scars fade from his face and arms. When she removed her hand from his arm, Daniel Bordeaux looked like he was twenty-five.

"Amazing, this is truly amazing."

"You're telling me, you are a complete knockout."

"What…what do you mean I'm a knockout? You're the one who changed."

"Not just me. You've changed too. If I may be so pretentious as to ask, how old are you?"

"I'm not ashamed to say I am thirty...well I will be thirty-nine in a few months."

"Really, you'll have a hard time making anyone else believe it. You look like you're at the most nineteen."

"If you were trying to get to a woman's heart; flattery is a good place to start. I may look younger than my thirty-nine years, but I certainly don't look nineteen. However you do look like you are twenty-five now."

"Let's go look in the mirror."

Together they went into the bathroom and looked into the mirror over the vanity. Both were amazed with the results of their little experiment. "Oh my," Jaime said as Daniel stood silently.

"This could be a problem," Daniel said.

"Problem, what problem? How could this be anything but a blessing? How old did you say you were? Fifty something?"

"I never said...but I'm in my sixties...but now I look like I'm in my early twenties. No way in hell I'm going to get anyone to believe I'm an over the hill homicide detective for the ABI. I bet no one will even recognize me. How in the hell am I going to?

"What get some to believe it's really you?"

"Yeah, that could be a problem."

"Don't go back to your old life."

"And do what? What can…what would I do?"

"Daniel have you ever been married?"

"No, why?"

"So you've spent every dime you've ever made? You don't have any savings?"

"Well to tell you the truth, I've never spent even a fourth of my income in any year. I…well monetarily I would never have to worry about a thing. My income from my real estate holdings will support me. I own a few apartment complexes in Birmingham."

"On a policeman's salary?"

"No, I saved my money and almost thirty years ago began buying Birmingham Real Estate. I purchased a small duplex apartment building first, living in one side and renting out the other. Through the years I have continued to buy properties. I've never bought property just to be the owner of it. I have always bought income producing property."

"So you owe quite a bit of money too then?"

"No, if you pull up my credit history, all you'll find is my name and a social security number. I've always paid cash for everything I've ever bought. I used the income from one property to buy the next property. Right now my real estate holdings bring me in an income of almost…well more than twenty times what the state of Alabama pays me for being an investigator."

"You must live like a king down in Birmingham."

"Truth be known, I live in a small one bedroom apartment in one of my complexes. I don't even own a car, or a television. My whole life has been tracking down bad guys. I guess I…well I never really cared what anyone thought of my lifestyle. The people in the complex I live in don't even know I own it."

"So you could walk away from the whole thing, and receive a very good income. Could you run your holdings from a remote place? Or maybe you could sell them?"

"And do what?"

"I don't know. We'll figure something out."

Daniel suddenly felt like Jaime was trying to tell him something. Did she say we? Did she mean Jaime and Daniel together? He could do worse than to end up with a beautiful resourceful young woman with the mind of this one. Three weeks ago, he had thought he was happy, but now he realized he hadn't been happy. Daniel Bordeaux had never been happy in his entire life. Daniel Bordeaux had always been exactly as he was in the Marines, a survivor. Jaime Iron offered him something he'd never had. If he was reading the situation right Jaime Iron was offering him the chance for real happiness.

Daniel once again confirmed his earlier thoughts as to his life in the ABI being over. No one there would believe he was who he claimed to be anyway. But his real estate holdings and other portfolios could be disposed of remotely. Very few people he did business with had ever seen him personally. His brokers had only spoken to him on the phone. He could run everything from Colbert Heights as efficiently as he could from Birmingham.

Chapter Eighteen

Outside they could still hear the storm raging as the angel Azrael made good on her word. Daniel listened as the howling winds gradually moved away from the home. Even though the winds were moving away, he was sure the sound outside was deafening. Daniel looked down at his watch and saw it was now closing in on nine p.m. It surprised him to see the storm outside still raging almost five hours after it started.

"I've put Lavis to bed," Jaime said as she sat down on the couch beside him. "I don't know how well she'll sleep tonight, but she is really tired. She's had a long day. This is the first time in recent memory she didn't get a nap."

Daniel wondered where this was going. He felt—as a result of Jaime's healing powers—better than he had in more than forty years. Daniel didn't really know when he did it, but he reached over and pulled Jaime closer.

After a few minutes, Jaime looked up at him and kissed him gently and apprehensively. She wasn't sure why she did this, but it felt right. Daniel responded with the patience Arnold had shown her, not pushing himself on her, not demanding at all, but willing to accept whatever she was willing to offer.

The kissing evolved into a heavy petting session which ended up in the bedroom. Daniel carried Jaime down the hall to the bedroom kissing her all the way down the hall. When he got to the bedroom, he silently opened the door turning on the light as he crossed into the bedroom.

Jaime wriggled out of Daniel's arms when he was about to lay her on the bed. Daniel could tell she hadn't been with many men, and suddenly was afraid he had overstepped his bounds. This wasn't a Vietnamese whore. What was he thinking? A woman as elegant as Jaime Iron wouldn't want an old gruff policeman, would she? He thought all of these things not realizing he wasn't an old gruff policeman anymore. Now he was a young man with a hard body.

Jaime felt a little apprehension as Daniel carried her down the hall into the bedroom. Did she really want this to happen? It took her only a moment to decide yes she really did want this to happen. She still saw in her heart the man she had first met only four days ago. These last four days had been almost unbelievable, but even before Daniel Bordeaux had become the young hunk who was carrying her down the hall; she had been physically and emotionally attracted to him. With these new changes, she was even more attracted to him.

Daniel thought Jaime was going to tell him she couldn't do this when she began to slowly undress. When Jaime stood before him as naked as a jaybird, she rapidly began to undress him. Their eagerness intensified as Daniel's clothes hit the floor all around him.

146

Whatever Jaime Iron may have lacked in experience, she more than made up for with enthusiasm. Daniel pulled her down to the bed and began to kiss her hungrily. Jaime kissed him back with unchecked passion. They made love as if they were the last hope of humanity. Daniel did things for Jaime she wouldn't have believed was possible only an hour before. Jaime's inexperience didn't at all quell Daniel's desire for her. Inexperience could be remedied by practice, and he intended to provide her as much practice as she deemed necessary. But for all of Jaime's inexperience, she was without a doubt the best partner he had ever found. Maybe it was because suddenly he was feeling something he had never felt before...was it? Could it possibly be he loved this woman? How could he—ever the professional bachelor—love this woman so completely after only a few days? Daniel didn't know the answer to the question; he only knew what he felt right now.

It was less than an hour until daylight when the lovers finally spent from an incredible night of passion drifted off to sleep. Daniel dreamed for the first time in his life of a beautiful wedding in which he was the groom and the gorgeous blonde bombshell Jaime Iron was wearing the white gown of the bride.

The dream started beautifully but ended horribly. The wedding ceremony was interrupted by a vision of perfection in the form of the angel Azrael. The angel swung her sword decapitating the wedding party one by one while Daniel Bordeaux stood by helpless.

Daniel looked on as the angel tied up the young form of Lavis Ann and before a cheering crowd lit a fire in the church and stood over the vulnerable young girl and plunged a sword heated white hot into her eye. Lavis Ann arched her back in pain as the angel's sword pushed into her brain. When the deed was complete, Daniel watched as the angel carved a strip of meat out of the back of the young girl's body and tossed it onto a fire which had appeared in the pulpit of the church.

Daniel felt a tugging at his pants leg and turned to see the other twenty-seven girls behind him. Their eyes were burnt out and as one they were asking him why he had not protected them. "Why did you not protect us?" They cried, "If you can't protect the little children, you don't deserve to live." Then as one, they began to rip and tear at his flesh.

Daniel woke screaming. He remembered the dream vividly and knew immediately there was a lesson to be learned from it. This vision may not happen literally, but if he didn't do something to stop the angel, Lavis Ann would soon be under the knife of the angel Azrael.

Daniel made a decision; his decision would shape the future more than he would realize. Daniel from this moment on would do whatever it took to destroy the angel of death, even if it meant losing his own life. If it meant losing his eternal soul—something he didn't believe he had only yesterday—he was willing to pay

the price to protect Jaime Iron, a woman who had
become his lover, and her young girl.

Daniel rose quietly and walked into the bathroom,
looking at his watch as he walked. It was five thirty.
It was his normal time to get up. After Daniel had
finished his morning bathroom business he walked
back into the bedroom looking at Jaime's perfect
form lying atop the tangled damp bedclothes. Jaime
Iron was an incredible woman, both inside and
outside the bedroom. He quietly put on his clothes
and walked out into the living room.

Daniel had to plan. Plans were what kept you alive
when you were a battle zone. That's what this was.
This was a battle zone. Daniel didn't know what he
was facing, not exactly anyway. Battles and wars
weren't always fought with perfect understanding of
the enemy's capabilities. Sometimes you only had to
go with the gut feeling. Right now his gut feeling was
that it would be him, not Jaime Iron that killed the
angel Azrael.

Daniel walked over to the place where he had seen
Jaime un-belt what he thought would be the angel's
sword. Daniel felt for the sword inch by inch until he
touched something he couldn't see. Running his hand
up what felt like a jeweled sheath Daniel finally
found what he knew to be the hilt of the sword. When
Daniel grasped the hilt of the sword, it became visible
to him.

Daniel was awed by the beauty of the weapon. There were collectors who would pay hundreds of thousands even millions of dollars for a sword with no powers half as beautiful as this one was. He removed it from the sheath and marveled at the light which seemed to come from within the sword. It was as if someone had captured starlight and somehow incorporated it into this beautiful razor sharp weapon.

Soon the angel Azrael would pay for the destruction of so many young lives. Daniel would see to it Azrael paid, in blood if angels bleed.

Chapter Nineteen

"You get the hell down there and find out what in God's name is going on. I want pictures of this blast zone as they're calling it. You get to Daniel and find out what in the hell he saw last night."

"Yes sir," Ben answered.

"What's up with the pictures? I understand we can't copy them?"

"Well no sir, that's not entirely accurate. We have no problem copying the ...well we have no idea how to duplicate the 3-d, but we can make a perfectly good photocopy of the photograph except the lady in the photo...well she comes out as a bright spot on the copy. Everything the techs have tried has been unsuccessful. We don't know what else to try."

"Have you tried getting one of our or the FBI's sketch artists to draw a picture of the woman? Surely we have someone who can draw a competent sketch we can send to the papers and TV, don't we?"

"Well...yes I guess we should."

"Then you...no I'll make sure it gets done you get up to Colbert Heights and find out what the hell's going on up there. My people are telling me not even viruses survived the storm. They're telling me nothing is alive in the path of the storm; at least we hope it was a storm. They're telling me this so called tornado pulled rocks out of the ground, storm shelters up and totally destroyed everything. I don't know how it's possible, but you make sure you get a report from Daniel Bordeaux. I want to know what he saw."

"Do you want me to drive up there? I think everyone; no I know every member of the press is there. You probably can't get within fifteen miles of Colbert Heights, even in a police car."

"No, I'll call out to the helo-pad. Take the chopper. I want you back here before dark with some answers."

"Yes sir."

Ben started to walk out of the office. As he walked through the bull pen Captain Gaines came out of his office. "Hey Ben, one more thing, I want you to take pictures of the place. I understand Jaime Iron's place is untouched. I want pictures of her place. I don't know why I feel I need them, but I feel somehow they will be instrumental to catching this Sacrificial Lambs idiot. It's a feeling, call it a hunch, but sometimes my hunches have played out very well. I don't think I'll be wrong on this one. Somehow this is connected to the killer."

"I don't see how this..."

"Neither do I at this precise time, but I think it will become clear in the near future."

Chapter Twenty

Azrael watched as thousands of people combed the path of destruction she had wrought only a few short hours before. They would try to explain this with science. She had no doubt the government of this place would come up with some kind of unbelievable explanation, but in the years to come no one would effectively explain what had happened here.

As Azrael watched the researchers comb through the now fertile soil in what only yesterday was a thriving small town she got an idea. What better way to increase the fear than to begin to systematically kill the persons walking around on the path she had taken the night before.

Azrael drew her sword and walked up to a man walking around with a clicking machine used to measure radiation. Taking her sword she pushed it into the heart of the man. When the man had died, one of the hosts of angels was there to immediately escort him away to his proper place. Azrael walked among the people, killing them one by one until the rest of the population noticed people were dropping dead all over the place.

A panic ensued with people trampling other people in a concerted effort to remove themselves from the blood enriched soil. Azrael took no notice of the panic and proceeded to kill more than five-hundred of the persons standing in the path she had taken last night around Jaime Iron's home. Seventeen minutes after she had killed the first man with the Geiger counter Azrael once again stood by herself looking at the Iron home. She made the decision she would kill anyone who dared to come into the mile circle surrounding the home of Jaime Iron.

Once again Azrael wondered why the girl was so fortunate as to be protected by the Archangel Michael. Never in Azrael's reign as the supreme angel of death had a person or persons been protected by an Archangel. Could it be the Heavenly Father had something special planned for the little girl? Azrael once again wished for the Father's guidance, but her wishes were not answered.

Why, wondered Azrael, *does God hold counsel with all of the other archangels, but never with me? Why was she, Azrael left out of heaven? Why could she not at least once a month or even once a year, stand and bask in the glow of the heavenly father for a short time?* Azrael thought she knew the answer. Yet even with her almost infinite wisdom she wasn't sure.

Azrael thought back to the time when she had—like Daniel and Jaime been human. Azrael had once been a mother herself. She had not always been the angel of death. This had been inflicted upon her as punishment for the murder of the former angel of death. Azrael had been the supreme angel of death for more years than she cared to count—for more years than humans could number. Azrael had once been mortal, but this had been long before the great flood. Azrael was one of the original humans, a daughter of Adam. She was a sister to Cain, effectively her grandfather *was* God. This was long before the confusion of tongues, long before the tower of Babel. Once she had been a mother to a child and had killed the angel sent to retrieve her daughter's soul. He had been the original Azrael, not born of a human, but created by none other than God himself.

Azrael had been cursed for the murder of an angel, one of God's messengers sent only to do his job, God's bidding. Upon finding the Angel of Death standing over her daughter, beside the house where it was immediately obvious her daughter had fallen off of the roof, the current Azrael—her name a word unpronounceable in modern English but loosely translated to Miranda *(Admirable and Beautiful)* Miranda had quickly removed the sword hanging from the belt of the angel, blaming Azrael for her daughter's death, and beheaded him.

A chorus of angels immediately feeling one of their numbers had been somehow killed came to see what, or who had killed the beloved angel. Azrael had been one of the beloved angels who delivered a human's soul to the heavenly court. Then unlike now there had been no phobia concerning death. Everyone knew when a human died they simply went to heaven to be with God. However even then there was a sorrow when the transcendence occurred. People were missed and this was what had caused the murder of the angel sent to retrieve the soul of Miranda's little girl.

Immediately Miranda knew she had committed a terrible wrong and had got down on her knees and began to pray. She prayed for forgiveness for killing one of God's most beautiful creatures, but forgiveness was not to be had this day. God himself had walked on the face of the earth that day looking for his fallen angel. Finding Miranda standing over the angel, holding the angel's sword he had spoken a few simple words.

"Miranda born of Eve, this day you are content with what you are—a murderer—that you shall remain until you like your predecessor are beheaded. Such as you are now you shall remain until your life is taken in combat by a stronger will than yours. There has never been a fear of death, but now because of your transgression you shall become one of the most feared and hated of all the angels. Be content with what you are for that you shall remain—ALONE— until another makes the same transgression or until the second coming of my son the Christ."

The transgression had happened so many years ago. Azrael weary from her duties only wished it would end. Azrael prayed every day God would take her burden from her, but so far in the many millennia which followed, her prayers had been unanswered.

Azrael would like nothing better than to give this *Job* to another.

Chapter Twenty-One

"So now are you gonna be my daddy? Now I know my mommy likes you, no one 'cept Mommy an me an Connie has ever slept in mommy's room. Well I guess my daddy slept in her room once, but I don't 'member him."

"What?"

"Mommy's bedroom, I know you slept in mommy's bedroom last night. Does this mean you'll be my daddy? I really want a daddy."

Daniel looked down at the little girl and wondered, *where in God's name did you come from?* Lavis had simply, as quiet as a church mouse, walked up behind him and started quizzing him. How had she known Daniel had slept in the room with her mother? "Where did you get the idea I slept in the room with your mother?"

"'Cause the covers were all rumpled up. My mommy doesn't rumple the covers up. When she gets outta the bed it almost looks like no one's slept in it. I think you rumpled the covers. Bed looks like it does when me an Connie sleep with her. It's all mussed up."

Man this girl was sharp. Daniel wished he had a few detectives as observant as this little girl was. "Because the bed's mussed up doesn't mean I slept in there. Maybe your mommy had a bad dream and mussed up the bed herself."

"Or maybe you mussed it up. What're you doin' with the sword? You're not gonna hurt me and mommy with it are you?"

"You can see the sword?"

"O'course I can see it. Mommy was carryin' it yesterday. Now you've got it."

"You've been able to see it the whole time?"

"Yeah, ever since Michael gave it to her."

"You saw the angel too?"

"Not zactly."

"What do you mean not exactly?"

"I din't see the angel zactly, but I heard what he told my Mommy in my head. An when we were coming home in the police car that night from the motel up in 'tucky I could see it hanging on a belt 'round her waist."

"I'm curious, how did you get back here from Kentucky?"

"We rode in the police car."

"What car?"

"The one we rode up to 'tucky in. The one that smelled like someone used the bathroom in it, that's the car we came back in."

"Then why isn't it here?"

"'Cause when we got here it disappeared. I guess it went back to 'tucky."

"It disappeared?"

"Yeah, it faded like someone turned it off, you know like you turned off the TV, it went away."

"So you're saying it disappeared? When did it disappear?"

"Soon as Mommy turned her back it disappeared."

"Do you know where it went?"

"I guess it went back to 'tucky, since you came back in it. Wasn't it in 'tucky when you left? Isn't that the same car we rode home in there in the drive?"

Why was he having this conversation with the little girl? She asked more questions in two minutes than you could answer in four years. Why this, who's that, ifin I do this what will happen why'd you do that? Over and over it was an unanswerable stream of questions.

"You never did answer my question. Are you going to be my new daddy?"

"I don't know. Now could you hush and let me think, I can't concentrate with you yapping around my feet like a little terrier."

Daniel saw as soon as he said this he had said the wrong thing.

"Why're you yelling at me?" asked Lavis with tears in her eyes. "I never yell at you, an I'm not running around your feet like a tarantula. I hate spiders."

Exasperated Daniel looked down at the tear stained face of the beautiful young girl. *Damnit*, Daniel thought, *I think I would rather tackle a bear naked in the woods with a willow switch as to try to converse with this child. It seems like every time I talk to her she ends up crying.* "Baby I'm not meaning to yell at you. It's how I talk sometimes. I'm not mad at you; I really need to think. I'm trying to figure out how to protect you from…"

"Oh, why didn't you say so instead of telling me I was a yapping tarantula? I can help you protect me an Mommy. I know what you need to do."

"So…you know what I need to do?" Daniel asked her with a sarcasm missed by the little girl."

"It's simple, you need to take the sword you're carrying an kill the angel. You've gotta kill Azrael like Michael said."

"You think I can kill the angel Azrael with this sword?" Daniel suddenly didn't know why he had asked the little girl about killing something.

Lavis brightened and said, "Yeah, the angel said you had to remove her head. I think you sneak up behind her and cut off her head lik'n you were cutting down weeds in the garden."

"Didn't the angel say your mother had to do it?"

"No, the angel said the only way to kill an angel was to cut off her head. I don' think he said who had to do it."

Daniel stood for a moment and wondered if the sword worked for him like it did for Jaime. Well there was one way to find out. Daniel grasped the hilt of the sword and thought of Captain Gaines. In an instant he was standing before the Captain's desk as the Captain looked down at his paperwork. Apparently Captain Gaines hadn't heard him come in, or flash in or appear or whatever he had accomplished. Before the Captain could or did notice he was there, Daniel grasped the handle of the sword once again and thought of little Lavis Ann. Before he could really finish the thought, he was once again standing looking down at the little girl. Pity he hadn't had something like this in the war, this would have made finding the enemy a lot easier. All he would have had to do was think of the enemy, and ...well no Jaime said he had to think of a particular person for it to work.

Daniel thought of the Al-Qaeda network and was rewarded with nothing. However when he thought of the tall man associated with the destruction of World Trade Center he suddenly was standing inside a makeshift hospital room which seemed to be located inside a cave of some sort. Daniel looked down at the tall thin man inhabiting the hospital bed. Daniel had heard this man had a severe case of Diabetes and it seemed he was very sick. But even in what seemed to be the final throes of death, this man radiated evil. The man raised his head and looked directly into Daniel's eyes. Daniel could see this man's hatred of him and all he represented. Somehow Daniel had known the Al-Qaeda leader hadn't been killed by a SEAL team.

Without a second thought, Daniel raised the sword above his head and with a swift sure stroke removed this evil man's head, cleaving not only through his neck but through the entire bed on which he lay. The bed crashed to the floor and Daniel knew soon there would be people coming, everyone here had to have heard the crash of the bed.

This was not the first time Daniel had ever killed, certainly not the first time he had ever killed with malice, but it was the first time it had ever felt so satisfying. This man had been directly responsible for the death of more than two thousand of Daniel's countrymen. To kill in war was one thing, but to plan the death of more than two thousand innocent civilians was another thing entirely. For this crime Daniel quickly had been the judge jury and executioner.

While this had not been the first time Daniel had ever taken a man's life, it was the first time he had ever seen firsthand the aftereffects of the event. Daniel watched as the man's spirit rose to a place slightly more than a foot above his now headless body. The malevolent spirit hovered with an anger Daniel could feel even in death. The spirit could do no harm now and as Daniel watched a pit opened up in the center of the room immediately to his right and two (demons?) sprang from the pit, wrapped the terrorist in a set of heavy chains and dragged the spirit screaming into a pit which was belching copious amounts of horrible smelling black smoke and a bright blue flame that looked hotter than any blowtorch.

Standing not more than three feet from the hole, Daniel should have been able to feel the heat from the immense blowtorch, but the room felt as cool as a cave should. Daniel watched as the pit closed behind the demons and the malevolent spirit. The screams from the man Daniel had murdered mingled with a cacophony of other screams until it was unrecognizable. As Daniel stood there looking at the dead body of the former leader of the terrorist faction, Daniel felt only sorrow for the misguided man. Killer though he may have been even a man as cynical as Daniel thought no-one deserved to be punished like he knew this man would be.

Daniel dropped the terrorist's head and thought of Jaime. As soon as the thought was completed, Daniel stood before the foot of the bed watching the exhausted lady sleep. Quietly he crept out of the bedroom and into the hallway closing the door quietly behind him.

Daniel looked down at the sword, expecting it to be dripping with the blood of the slain, but it was as clean as if it had not been used. Sheathing the sword Daniel walked back down the hall and into the living room where Lavis Ann had another thousand questions for him.

Chapter Twenty-Two

"I wouldn't do it sir," one of the Colbert County deputies told Ben McElroy. "Everybody who's walked out into the circle in the past two hours has died instantly. Right now we can't even send someone out to collect the bodies."

"What do you mean everybody?"

"Jus' what I said I don't know what the deal is, but everyone who steps foot in that bare spot dies within a minute."

"You don't understand; I really need to talk to Daniel Bordeaux. The Captain sent me . . ."

"*No,* you don't understand; I'm not keeping you from walking out there. Walk your skinny white ass out there...you won't make three steps into the circle...I ain't stopping you. If you're too stupid to look at the dead bodies out there in the circle of mud and see all the dead bodies scattered then I guess when we figger out how to get em out the funeral director can wipe your stupid ass a before he sticks you in a box. Can you see all the bodies scattered across the circle?"

Ben looked out across the bare circle of mud and for the first time saw more bodies than he cared to count. There must be hundreds of them. "What happened to them?" he asked.

"No one knows yet, all we know right now is if you happen to walk into the circle you don't live for the next five minutes even if you can get back out."

"Is it some kind of ...?"

"I don' told you we don' know...we don' know if it's a disease, heart attack...what? What we know is if they walk out there they die...dead, just fall over and don' even kick."

"The Captain's not going to like this. He sent me out here to talk to Daniel and..."

"If I was you, I'd tell him to come out here and talk to Daniel his damn self. I know you really like your job but it ain't worth dying for. Least over something as stupid as walking into a circle that has killed everyone in the last hour. Wait for a little while, the Government has a team of NBC people on the way out here."

"NBC, what's NBC?"

"Nuclear Biological and Chemical. They've decided it must be some kind of contaminant, so they're sending a team out here to check it out."

"I wonder how long it's gonna take. It'll probably be hours yet before they get here won't it?"

"I don' know they talked like they would be here in a few minutes, said they were flying a team out of Redstone Arsenal. Shouldn't be long."

As the state investigator and the deputy sheriff were finishing the conversation, to their east they heard the helicopters coming. In slightly less than two minutes from the time they first heard the helicopters, three large helicopters were landing in a cloud of dust in a field not more than one hundred yards from the two police officers.

Ben watched as three teams of four men (or women Ben couldn't tell in the space suits the teams were wearing) jumped out of the choppers and began unloading equipment. When the (whatever it was) was unloaded the choppers once again took to the air. Moments later three more helicopters landed, this time with soldiers in full Mopp gear. The soldiers began setting up a perimeter.

Chapter Twenty-Three

Daniel heard the choppers long before he could see them. They sounded exactly the same as they had sounded in 'Nam. He walked out onto the porch and looked out over the horizon. Four of them, he wondered what the government would be doing out here. Yeah, Azrael's tornado had to have been one strange looking weather pattern on anyone's radar. But there was nothing to be found out by looking at the one surviving house, was there?

Daniel wandered out to the edge of the property, where the beautifully landscaped yard became a field of mud. As he looked out over what now looked like a large recently plowed field, he for the first time saw the hundreds of bodies lying out there in the field. Had they been Jaime's neighbors? If they were, it seemed like all of her neighbors were male and wore some type of business suit. No, they had to be researchers of some kind.

Wondering why the government was sending four big choppers out to a natural disaster, Daniel remembered the field glasses in the trunk of the police car. He went back to the car, opened the trunk and rummaged around until he found the large set of binoculars. Daniel went back to the place he had been standing recently and opened the case and removed the glasses, took the protective caps off the lenses and brought them up to his eyes. As Daniel watched, the passengers began to exit the chopper, and Daniel saw they had on the space suits he knew were for going into areas deemed to have contaminants of some kind. What in the hell were they thinking? Did they think this was some kind of weapon of mass destruction? If it was why would there be a house in the middle of it?

As soon as the (Drs.?) were finished with their exodus of the chopper, the helicopters leapt into the air, and within two minutes had vanished from sight. Before they had completely vanished, Daniel saw there were three more helicopters coming this way. He once again raised the field glasses to his eyes and watched as a group of soldiers exited the plane wearing their Military protective covering. They did think this was a blast sight of some kind. Or more likely they didn't know exactly what the hell they were dealing with and wanted to be prepared for everything and anything.

He knew exactly what they were doing; they were getting ready to completely isolate the area. In less than one hour the entire area within five miles would be quarantined, and no one would be allowed in or out. He scanned the area looking at the myriad of people gathered outside the circle of what looked like fresh plowed ground. All at once he saw what had to be Ben. Even through the powerful binoculars Daniel couldn't completely be sure, but he felt it was his partner. Unconsciously Daniel touched the handle of the sword while thinking of his young partner.

Faster than the blink of an eye, faster even than Daniel could even take the thought back, he was standing directly in front of Ben.

"What…where did…Where did you come from," asked a startled Ben McElroy. "You look familiar, do I know you?"

"Of course you know me, I…uh," Daniel had forgotten about the change in his appearance. He didn't look like the old man his partner knew. "Aren't you that cop? You're the cop looking for the Sacrificial Lambs killer, aren't you?"

Ben looked at the twenty something man standing in front of him and felt like he knew him, if he didn't know better, by the timber of this man's voice he would think this was, no, it couldn't possibly be? "Daniel? What in the God's name has happened to you? It is you isn't it? You look so, uhm…you look so young. What on earth did you do to yourself?"

"You wouldn't believe it if I told you. I think you need to get these people out of here. This is not the place for them right now, it's still too dangerous. They could get killed, I'm pretty sure if they walk out into the circle they'll…"

"I'm sure they'll be fine, whatever is out there killing…well those suits will protect them from any contagion."

"No, nothing on this earth will…can protect them from Azrael. She's not like anything they've ever seen before, well it's nothing anyone except me and Jaime's ever seen before and lived. She'll kill them; space suits or not."

"What's out there? And how did you get so young?"

"First things first, what's out there is the angel of death, Azrael. She…I'm pretty sure she's killing anything that dares to walk into the circle."

"Dan, what the hell are you talking about? What's this angel of death crap?"

"The angel of . . . well Azrael is her name, and she's the sacrificial lambs killer. She's the one who did this. Jaime's remaining little girl is the next one on her list, and she's pissed because Lavis is being protected by Michael, he said she's special and…"

"Whoa, whoa, hold on you're not talking about an angel, a literal angel are you?"

"Yes, an angel is exactly what I'm talking about. Azrael is the angel of death. I think she's went a little crazy, and she is killing . . ."

"You mean to tell me it's a real angel? Do you know how crazy you sound? Dan do you know how…?" Once again Ben looked at his partner and saw how young he looked. How in the hell did a man on the horizon of retirement suddenly look like he was in his twenties? "Dan if it's you I could have you held for psychiatric review for even thinking such a thing."

Don't call me crazy Ben; and I'm not going anywhere with you... "don't start with me, I don't have time. I need you to do one thing and one thing only, I need you to find whoever is commanding this unit and do whatever you have to short of shooting him to keep all of his people out of the circle. If you don't...well Azrael will take care them. I assure you she is one serious character, not someone or rather something to be trifled with. Azrael is an immensely powerful being with unlimited unimaginable power. She...well look around you," Daniel swept his hand toward the Iron home, "she did it all."

"Are you saying an angel did all of this?"

"That's exactly what I'm saying. No matter what these people look for or think they've found, I've seen the truth, and it is almost unbelievable. If you don't want these people to die, get them out of here. Don't let them cross into the circle."

Before Ben could say anything else Daniel touched the handle of the sword and thought of little Lavis Iron and once again before he could even take the thought back he was standing back in the Iron home.

Chapter Twenty-Four

Ben fought through the throng of Military personnel until he found someone who seemed to be in command. "Colonel, sir could I have a word with you?"

"Who in the hell are you?"

"I'm special investigator Benjamin McElroy of the Alabama Department of Investigation, and I…"

"Don't have time to talk to you now son, I'll see your superiors get a report." The Colonel promptly turned his back and began walking away giving orders to his underlings. "Now you get your…"

"Colonel," Ben grabbed the colonel's shoulder I really need to have a word with you, this isn't about any report. If you send your men out there they will be killed."

"Son, don't you put your hands on me ever again. I think I know how to handle a containment problem. This is some kind of well it's not like anything we've ever seen before, but we'll figure it out. Now I've got a job to do, excuse me sir."

Once again the colonel tried to walk away, and once again Ben grabbed one of his shoulders. This time though, the colonel was not polite as he had been. "Boy I told you one time not to touch me. I'll have you arrested for interfering with a federal investigation. MPs get this clown out of here. Escort him to someplace the hell away from me, I don't have time . . ."

Ben saw two formidable looking young men with MP stenciled on the camouflage covering of their Kevlar helmets coming toward him. Ben knew without a doubt in an instant the two MPs would have him in their custody, and he would probably be charged as the colonel had said with obstructing a federal investigation. No, he may be arrested for something, but it would not be minor. He stood for only a second, making up his mind, and did something he thought he would never do.

Colonel Hart heard the hammer back on what he knew was a nine millimeter semi-automatic handgun of some description, probably if he remembered right it was either a Beretta or a Colt. "Stop right there Colonel or it will be the last step you'll take." Ben heard the M-16's the MPs were carrying each chamber a round. "Colonel your boys may kill me, but if they do, you'll never get a chance to hear what I've got to say."

"Easy boys, let's hear what this man's got." Colonel Hart turned around and for the first time really looked at Ben McElroy. "Well speak up son, I don't have all day."

Ben looked at the tired time worn face of the man who would never make general. Colonel Hart had a stern expression. It was obvious this was a man with little time for bullshit. The Colonel was rail thin, and it was apparent he had reached the pinnacle of his career, well not the pinnacle, but it was as far as he really wanted to go. Colonel Hart was a man in his sixties, and like Daniel Bordeaux had the eyes of a killer. They were eyes which had seen death dealt by the owner of the body in which they lay. As Ben watched, these eyes became cold and calculating, Ben could almost see the brain working behind them. It was almost as if they were real wheels and cogs spinning behind those cold calculating eyes. "Well son speak your peace, I've already said this what seems like a dozen times I've got a job to do, and I damn well am going to do it."

"Colonel if you send any of those men out into the patch of bare ground, they will die. It won't matter what kind of protection they have or think they have, they will die as sure as I am standing here."

"I didn't realize you knew what the hell we were dealing with! Guess the God-Damned state of Alabama knows everything? If you already knew every-God-Damned thing why'd you call me? My men are the best trained in the world to deal with unknown substances. They have the best protection the U.S. Government can provide. So far, we've been able to determine this isn't any kind of nuclear threat, but we don't really understand what we're dealing with yet. I am one hundred percent sure we will figure out what we are dealing with, and I don't think some state cop needs to be telling me how to do my job.

Son how many unexplained phenomena have you ever dealt with? My guess is none. So don't be telling me one God-damned thing about my boys dying if they walk out into a little bare spot. I've seen bare spots before. Not this big mind you but I have seen my share of bare spots. The suits these boys are wearing will protect them from anything this or any other planet can throw at them. Now get out of my way and let me do my job, or I'll have my MPs shoot you and carry your carcass out and load it on a damned deuce and a half."

"Will your boy's suits protect them from the Angel of Death? Answer me Colonel; will they protect them from one of God's avenging angels?"

"What the hell are you talking about?"

"We have a state investigator in the house in the circle." Ben turned and pointed to the large home sitting in the circle, "Daniel Bordeaux. He tells me this is the work of one of Gods Angels, Azrael the angel of death. He told me not more than ten minutes ago anyone who wandered into the circle would be killed by Azrael. He seems to think she's pissed about another angel named Michael protecting the place. See we've been working on a serial killer case and..."

"You mean to tell me you think this is the work of an angel? Do you know how idiotic you sound? I guess I'll call General Cashion. I'll tell him that I can't do my job because a lunatic angel is protecting the spot they want the research done. You know what will happen then son? I'll be relieved of my command and probably sent for medical review. I've only got a few years left in this man's army son. It's been good to me, been a good life, and I damn well am not going to ruin a spotless military career with supernatural bullshit."

"Colonel I beg of you to reconsider what you're doing. According to Daniel Bordeaux, it would be suicide to send any of your men out into the circle. I've worked long enough with…"

Colonel Hart cut Ben off with the wave of a hand, "Mr.—I didn't catch your name but did you say Daniel Bordeaux, would he be former Gunnery Sergeant Daniel Bordeaux of the…"

"He was in Vietnam, I don't really know what unit he was in but I know from talking with a deputy sheriff—I believe the deputy's name is Tabb, maybe Ernie Tabb—but he said they were two of the most…"

"Ernie Tabb and Daniel Bordeaux; haven't thought of them for a long time. I really didn't know if either of them was still alive. You say Daniel Bordeaux is in the house?"

"You know him?" Ben finally let the gun fall to his side for a moment before putting it back into the holster hanging under his arm.

"Of course I know him. I was young Army lieutenant in Vietnam…the two of them saved our bacon more than once. Best damn sniper team I've ever seen. Daniel Bordeaux if it's the same one, and from what you tell me I have no doubts it is, is one of the few men in this entire world I would trust with my life and the life of my family. He's a good man, a solid man. So tell me exactly what did he say?"

Over the next few minutes Ben told the colonel the entire story from beginning to end. He told everything from finding the first girls sacrificed in the churches to the uncanny way the killer seemed to find the young girls no matter where they were. He ended with Daniel's new appearance, how he had suddenly appeared as if magic and telling him a story which was completely unbelievable.

When Ben was finished, Colonel Hart had doubt in his cold calculating eyes, but apparently none in his heart or mind. "If it's the case, and I find it hard to believe an Angel even if it is the Angel of Death Azrael would be doing something like this. . . I don't know what to believe at this point. You just told the craziest story I have ever heard, but on the other hand, if it is really Sergeant Bordeaux in the house, I have to believe what he has told you. The man is brutally honest and doesn't give a damn about anyone's feelings. He speaks the truth regardless what the truth is."

"So you believe me?"

"No I don't son, not a damn word of what you said I believe. Nothing against you personally mind you but I think the Angel what was his name Azrael? I think only Azrael himself can keep me from sending those boys out to do their job. Azrael may kill them. But they're soldiers; they get paid to risk their lives for their country."

"So you're telling me even if you believe Dan, you still are going to send the team out there anyway?"

"That's exactly what I'm telling you. The chain of command comes directly from the President. He wants to know what in the hell is going on down in this little part of Alabama and I am not going to call and tell him the Angel of Death is killing people. I may believe it if Sergeant Bordeaux came out here and told me himself, but even that's doubtful. You've said your peace son now get out of the way and let my people do their job."

Colonel Hart walked away giving orders the entire time. Looking out at the bare circle, Ben watched as the first of the men in the space suits walked out onto the bare ground. For a few moments nothing happened, and he began taking what looked like a hollow stick and pushing it into the ground filling it up with dirt. He took the hollow tube and dropped the contents into some kind of container held by another man in a space suit.

They had been out there for more than ten minutes when suddenly the man's head, space suit helmet and all rolled off onto the ground. Blood began to spray out of his neck where his head was attached at one time. As the lifeless body sank to its knees and fell forward the assistant holding the container began to scream, "No, no please don't we didn't know. Please don't." He ran out of the circle making it halfway across the grassy area between the perimeter and the bare circle before suddenly the man split halfway into two pieces. It looked as if a laser had cut him perfectly from the top of his head to his crotch.

"What in the name of Jesus Christ is going on?" bellowed the Colonel

Ben muttered under his breath, "I told you Colonel."

"Someone, Sergeant tell me what the hell is going on!"

A young woman wearing BDUs and the same helmet the rest of the MPs were wearing came running up to the colonel. "Permission to speak freely sir?" she requested as if she were scared to death of this man.

"Permission granted. Sergeant, tell me what the hell is going on! I want to know why there is no one out there in that circle getting me some goddamned answers to give to the general so he can inform the president."

"Sir, Doctors Chung and Mollahan were out in the bare spot when someone or something decapitated Doctor Chung. Doctor Mollahan ran out of the bare spot into the grass surrounding the . . . well halfway here, something cut him from the top of his head to his crotch splitting him perfectly in half."

"Did you see this Sergeant?"

"Yes sir."

"Inform me Sergeant. What killed my two doctors?"

"I don't know sir. I didn't see what did it, only the aftereffects of it."

"So you're telling me one of my doctors, his head fell off and the other one magically split in half?"

"Exactly sir."

"Sergeant, tell me what did this." Colonel Hart sounded calm, but Ben could see he was anything but calm. "Sergeant you have exactly five seconds to tell me exactly what killed my doctors."

"Sir, I saw it happen, but I don't know what killed them. I know what I saw, which was . . . well we didn't really see anything. It just happened, Doctor Mollahan was screaming, something like please don't we didn't know."

"Which was it Sergeant, was he screaming please don't we didn't know or was it something else."

"I'm pretty sure he was screaming please don't we didn't know, but it may have been something else, the helmet muffled his cries quite a bit and we were more than forty meters away still when he split in half."

"Very good Sergeant, move this perimeter back to a distance of five hundred meters. I want all these civilians out of here. Get General Burton at Campbell, tell him we have a class one containment problem here. Tell him we need everything the containment team has in the way of…tell him we need everything the God-damned U.S. government has to send out here. Get it done Sergeant…Why are you still standing there soldier? Get it done. I want the whole fuckin' Army here in twenty minutes. Do you understand me Sergeant?"

"Yes sir."

"Then why are you and the rest of these soldiers still standing around with their fingers in their asses. Get this cluster-fuck in gear."

Sergeant Bells snapped a quick salute and did a smart about face and began yelling orders to the various specialists and privates. When she had them moving the civilians out of the area, Ben saw her double time it to a Hum-Vee which must have been a command unit. It was covered with all manner of radio antennas from large whip style antennas to small satellite dishes.

Ben watched as the soldiers efficiently moved the civilian population toward their automobiles. Damn they were efficient, and they seemed to give less than a damn about the civil rights of the civilians or the first amendment rights of the press. Suddenly press credentials were worth exactly shit in this area.

To Ben's surprise, he found out his state credentials meant almost as much as the press credentials. An MP told him in no uncertain terms he would have to leave. He like the press and the civilian population would have to remain behind barricades the army was setting up at a distance of one mile from the bare spot.

"Sergeant! Sergeant! Where's my fucking Sergeant?"

"Right here Sir."

"Did you get Brigadier General Burton?"

"Yes sir."

"And?"

"Well sir he said the containment unit would be shipping out of Campbell in less than an hour."

"Very good Sergeant, the perimeter's moved back to five hundred meters?"

"Yes sir."

"Get every road blocked off for a distance of one mile from the perimeter. How many houses, how many families are within the secondary perimeter?"

"I don't know exactly several hundred people in the least, maybe forty families maybe more."

"It doesn't really matter if there are several thousand. I want them evacuated. We don't know what or who we are dealing with here. We have declared a state of emergency here; you are authorized to use any force necessary."

"Yes sir."

"Sir, may I ask a question?"

"You did Sergeant. But ask another if you must."

"Sir what about the family inside the circle what are we going to do with them?"

"Right now Sergeant, I don't think we're going to do anything. I'm not sure we can send anyone across the bare spot between us and them. Right now they'll have to wait where they are."

"I agree sir; they'll have to wait where they are. What about the press sir?"

"I'll let the press officer deal with them. Right now no one talks to the press at all. I don't want to see one word any of my people said quoted in whatever the local paper is. One more thing Sergeant, get me that state cop, the investigator. I want the investigator who told me the crazy story standing in front of me ASAP.

Chapter Twenty-Five

SHALL WE GATHER AT THE RIVER

WHERE MY ANGEL FEET HAVE TROD

WITH IT'S CRYSTAL TIDE FOREVER

FLOWING BY THE THRONE OF GOD

YES WE'LL GATHER AT THE RIVER

THE BEAUTIFUL THE BEAUTIFUL RIVER

GATHER WITH THE SAINTS AT THE RIVER

THAT FLOWS BY THE THRONE OF GOD

Daniel woke with the beautiful song being sung at a volume normally reserved for Metal Bands. He sat straight up in the bed as did Jaime. "What's that," he asked.

"I don't know," Jaime answered. Maybe this is the first day of Psychological torture. I will have to admit *Shall We Gather at the River* is one of my favorites."

"I understand, but does she have to sing it at a hundred and thirty decibels? I have to assume as beautiful as it sounds it has to be Azrael singing. I don't think the commander of the Army detail out there is piping it in to us do you?"

"No, it has to be Azrael. We're going to have to do something about her eventually I don't think we can stay here forever. Well I could, but I do think we will eventually have to have electricity again. Running water would be nice too."

"Yeah, I know. We're going to have to kill her, but how? You yourself said she is incredibly fast. I don't think you will be fast enough to kill her. Do you think I can?"

"Think you can what? Kill her? I don't know; have you ever used a sword before?"

"Not a sword exactly, but I did train with a master in Kendo years ago. I think I...no I know I remember most everything he taught me. Part of the training was with wooden swords, we were trained like the samurai of old. This training took six months or so, I think a little practice with this sword will bring it back. Hell I think even if you had never trained with any sword, this particular sword would make you an expert. I think the power of God is infused into the sword. Not all of God's power, only enough to do wonderful things."

"Yeah, wonderful things like transport yourself instantly with a thought and the power to heal what ails you, the power of the fountain of youth."

"Aren't these new bodies wonderful?"

Jaime suddenly teared up and without warning began to cry in great sobs. "I wouldn't have traded Connie Kay for...for...I want my little girl back. I want everything to go back to being normal again. I just want to be my children's mother again. I want my normal boring life back. I want the life I had back. I want my predictable, boring life in which I wasn't confined to my home. My life where I had neighbors and not a circle of mud surrounding my home. I want to send my daughter back to school. I want to stand at the end of the driveway waiting for her to get off the school bus. I want to bake cookies and attend stupid little school plays. I want..." Jaime suddenly broke down completely and sobbed uncontrollably.

Daniel may have been an old man when he first met Jaime, but that didn't mean he had any idea what to tell her. He didn't have any idea what to say, so he probably did the best thing he could have possibly done, he said nothing and pulled her tear stained face into his broad powerful chest and held her for a long time.

SHALL WE GATHER AT THE RIVER

WHERE CHILDRENS BLOODY FEET HAVE TROD

GATHER WITH THE DEAD AT THE RIVER

THAT RUNS WITH THE BLOOD OF THE SLAIN

YES WE'LL GATHER AT THE RIVER

THE BEAUTIFUL YET HORRIBLE RIVER

GATHER WITH THE DEAD AT THE RIVER

AND DROWN THEM IN THE BLOOD OF THE SLAIN

Almost at the same time Daniel and Jaime found themselves listening to the actual words of the song. This wasn't the beautiful hymn sung in churches each Sunday, this was a bastard version made up it would seem for Azrael's amusement. This version was made to torment Jaime.

SHALL WE GATHER AT THE RIVER

CONNIE KAY IS DOWN AT THE RIVER

SHE'S GATHERED WITH THE DEAD AT THE RIVER

THAT FLOWS WITH THE BLOOD OF THE SLAIN

YES WE'LL GATHER AT THE RIVER

THE BEAUTIFUL YET HORRIBLE RIVER

GATHER WITH CONNIE KAY AT THE RIVER

AND DROWN HER IN THE BLOOD OF THE SLAIN

SOON LAVIS ANN WILL REACH THE RIVER

THAT AWFUL AND BLOOD DARK RIVER

SOON LAVIS AND CONNIE WILL BE TOGETHER

FOREVER WITH THE REST OF THE SLAIN

YES LAVIS ANN WILL SEE THE RIVER

THAT BEAUTIFUL BLOOD DARK RIVER

SHE'LL GATHER WITH THE DEAD AT THE RIVER

AND I'LL DROWN HER IN THE BLOOD OF THE SLAIN

"Can you believe what she's singing?" Jaime said through sobs. "She's making fun of me. That bitch is making fun of the fact that she killed my daughter. *You wait you bitch...I'll kill you yet...You're a Dead Angel Bitch...I'll kill you if it is the last thing I ever do.*" Jaime was screaming this at the top of her lungs. Tears were streaming down her face and she was red either from all the crying or from pure unadulterated anger.

"Calm down Jaime, calm down. Anger will get you nowhere. That's exactly what she wants. Azrael wants you angry. She wants to torment you, she wants you to do something without thinking. Angry people make mistakes. If you really want to do as you said and kill her, we have to come with some kind of plan. It's like the old saying: most people don't plan to fail, they fail to plan. The only way we are going to defeat this magnificently powerful being is to out think her.

"We have to do something she wouldn't expect in a million years. I'm sure she has pretty much seen everything though, so we must do something even her superior mind cannot predict. We have to be unpredictable."

"Like what?" Jaime was starting to calm down somewhat, but that didn't seem to stop the torrent of tears that were running down her cheeks and had made her nightgown almost sheer by now. "I don't know yet. I have to talk to a few people. I know people who could literally plan for anything. There's a man I need to talk to, but I don't even know if he's still alive. There was an Army lieutenant when I was in Vietnam…Lieutenant James Hart, I wonder if he's still alive…I need to speak to him if he's still alive and I think I will need the help of Ernie Tabb."

"Who is Ernie Tabb?"

"Do you remember the day we first met?"

"Yeah, the day I had the cop convention in my yard, the day Azrael sent me the letter."

"Yes do you remember a frail looking black deputy for the Colbert County Sheriff's department?"

"Yeah, I think so. Was he a little guy? He's kind of old though isn't he?"

"Hey, hey he's younger than me."

"Sorry," Jaime said with a weak grin on her face."

Well Enoch Tabb is one of the most efficient killers who ever came out of a sniper school in the Vietnam Era. He's as deadly and as quiet as a cobra. If I can find Lieutenant Hart and Ernie Tabb and get them together, I think we can come up with a plan that will rid us of Azrael once and for all."

Jaime noticed the singing had stopped and it was deathly quiet. Outside there was no wind blowing, there was also—something to be grateful for—no singing. Jaime didn't know if that was a good sign, if Azrael was outside singing at the top of her lungs, at least they knew where she was. With Azrael, out of sight definitely didn't mean out of mind—at least not if you were smart.

Chapter Twenty-Six

"Where in God's name is that infernal noise coming from?" yelled Colonel Hart at Sergeant Christie Bells.

"I don't know sir. Maybe it's coming from the house…It could be…"

"What, do you think they have a sound system in the house capable of producing noise which would drown out a C-130 taking off?"

"Sergeant find out where this noise is coming from. I want to know what in the hell is going on here. This is the damnedest place I've ever been to. Circles killing my soldiers and now we're being woke up at six o'clock in the goddamned morning by something singing *Shall We Gather at the River* so loudly it seems it's coming from inside my head. I don't like God-damn hymns and I feel like if this keeps up our ears will be bleeding by the end of the day. Sergeant see if you can find me some earplugs and get earplugs into the ears of the rest of the soldiers."

"Yes sir," said Sergeant Bells as she double-timed it to a supply tent set up at the outside edge of the perimeter.

Before the sergeant could get to the tent, the singing stopped and it was deathly, almost eerily quiet. Colonel Hart looked out at the circle wondering if there was some way he could get to the civilians inside, or rather get them out to him. So far anyone or anything who had walked into the bare circle of mud

196

had led a very short life from that point forward. If they couldn't walk or drive any vehicle across the . . . What about flying? Could they possibly fly a chopper across the . . .

Colonel Hart walked back into his tent and went through his belongings until he found what he was looking for. The colonel walked back out with a pair of M-24 binoculars. He studied the area directly in front of the home, looking for a place to land a small helicopter. As he studied the landscape, he couldn't find a single place in the front yard or the side yards to land even the smallest helicopter. The yard was filled with large oak trees, power lines and other obstacles extremely dangerous to helicopters. Landing there would be impossible.

Somehow, the colonel thought, I've got to find a way to talk to the occupants of the home. If he couldn't land a chopper there, how could he get them out of there? What if he lowered a…that's it he would send a team across the circle in a chopper and rappel them down to the top of the house. They could get the occupants out of the house…maybe in a basket.

"Sergeant!" he screamed looking around for Christie Bells.

"Yes sir," she answered as she came running out of the supply tent.

"Get a team together I want a chopper in the air in fifteen minutes. Fly the team to the house over there and have them rappel down to the top of the house. I want a radio in that home in twenty minutes."

"Yes sir."

Ten minutes later a helicopter took off with a team of six, not including the pilots. They were wearing the new Battle Dress Uniforms with the built in body armor. The body armor didn't help though. Not even half-way across the circle, the helicopter stopped in mid-air and as everyone watched in horror, the helicopter seemed to be attacked by an un-seen lumberjack swinging a magnanimous axe.

The helicopter was cleaved into six different pieces and it looked as if someone shook out the occupants. As the soldiers fell, something cut them up as if they were in a colossal blender. When they hit the ground, they were nothing more than pieces of meat wearing what had once been the most sophisticated BDUs ever known to the Army.

"Ohmigod, did you see what happened sir?" Sergeant Bells said almost in an undertone. "I have never seen anything like that, have you?"

Colonel Hart was as awestruck as anyone standing watching the spectacle. Up until now, he thought he had seen every manner of death imaginable, but this . . . well this was completely impossible. Everything about this place, everything about this situation taxed his belief system in a way nothing ever had. He thought he had seen it all. He had been a commander in the U.S. Army's special investigations unit for more than ten years. He had given up the chance to become a general to become commander of this unit. He investigated everything from Alien abductions to well everything. He had seen things which would possibly never be known to the general public. Colonel Hart thought he had seen everything, until he saw a chopper sliced to pieces and its occupants cut into small slices of meat, like someone was planning on barbecuing them. He, Colonel James Madison Hart thought he had seen it all.

Suddenly as if by magic there was a tall muscular man wearing a suit slightly too large for him standing beside the Colonel. "Who...what are you?" the colonel asked uncertainly.

"Mornin' Colonel. I thought you would remember me, but it's been a long time. I'm," without giving him a chance to finish, the colonel said, "You're not, you can't be, are you...Sergeant Bordeaux?"

"Yes sir."

"Damn son you haven't changed one bit. You look exactly like you did thirty years ago. How is that possible? I know you have to be gettin' close to seventy now. I believe you're older than me, aren't you?"

"Yeah, Colonel I am, or rather I was until yesterday. I don't really want to go into the details of how I became a young man again here; I need your help."

Without further delay, Daniel pulled the Colonel into a tight embrace, touched the hilt of the sword and thought of Jaime.

Colonel Hart suddenly found himself standing in the living room of a modest but well-appointed home. "How did I…" before he could finish Daniel said, "wait here Colonel I'll be right back and vanished."

Only moments later he reappeared with an old man wearing the brown uniform of a Colbert County deputy.

Chapter Twenty-Seven

"Well the gang's all here," Jaime said as Daniel reappeared with Ernie Tabb. "While you guys get reacquainted, I'll make breakfast. Come on Lavis."

In a lot of households it would have been impossible to make breakfast, because no power equaled no stove or refrigeration. But when the power had gone off, Jaime in her vast wisdom had retrieved several large coolers from the garage and filled it with the frozen items from the freezer. She had packed the coolers tightly with all manner of frozen meats among other items. The Stove in the home was a propane model connected to a large tank outside. A simple model of efficiency, she soon had bacon and eggs frying and biscuits in the oven. While Jaime stood over the stove, Lavis got dishes out of the cabinet and set the table.

Jaime wasn't trying to listen in on their conversation, but the closeness of the kitchen prevented her from not overhearing.

"Well look at you. You didn't look as good thirty year ago. You look like a kid Dan," exclaimed Ernie Tabb. "How's it possible?"

"I don't have time to explain Ernie, and besides it's not why I brought you here."

"But you…you look like you did back when we were kickin' ass and forgettin' names."

"I know, let me show you something." Daniel reached out and took hold of the deputy's wrist. While he had Ernie's wrist in his hand he pulled the sword out of the sheath where it had been hanging at his waist. As raised the sword to waist level he willed himself to feel Ernie's pain. Daniel felt the compassion pouring out of his body and into the body of the frail deputy. He felt Ernie's spirit was damaged and as the compassion poured out of his body as it must have out of Jaime's only days ago, he watched as Ernie straightened and his skin changed from a faded gray to a luxurious shade of black. Ernie stood straighter and his muscles firmed under Daniel's hand. White hair became a chocolate color. Enoch's red rheumy eyes became the darkest shade of ebony and cleared up. In less than twenty seconds a fifty-something year old frail deputy became a young vibrant lithe well-muscled black man.

"What did you do to me? I feel better, but I can't see shit."

"Take off your glasses," Daniel said.

Ernie took off the thick Coke-bottle-bottom glasses, and stared around in observable wonder. "Oh my god, you've done fixed my eyes," he said in a voice riddled with astonishment.

"It's not all he fixed," said an equally astonished Colonel Hart. "Go look at yourself in the mirror Ernie."

While Ernie walked over to a mirror which hung on the living room wall and stared in wonder, Colonel Hart said, "Alright I'm sufficiently impressed. Tell me what I need to know."

"It'll have to wait gentlemen, breakfast's ready," said Jaime.

Thus two young men, an ancient looking Colonel, a beautiful young woman and a small girl sat down to a breakfast prepared by the beautiful young woman.

"Daniel, would you do the honor of saying grace?" Jaime asked before anyone could place as much as a single slice of bacon on their plate. The quintet bowed their heads respectfully as Daniel said a simple heartfelt prayer he wouldn't have believed he had in him to say only a few days ago.

When the prayer was finished, the colonel looked across the table at Daniel Bordeaux and said, "Now tell me about what just happened, and exactly what is going on here."

Before Daniel could answer the colonel's question Jaime broke in and said, "Colonel I don't mean to be rude, but the three of you have some planning to do, and I don't want it discussed over my breakfast table. It can wait a few minutes Colonel. At my table we only discuss pertinent family issues, and while technically this is a pertinent family issue, I don't want to discuss something as unpleasant as what this conversation will turn into. Do I make myself clear gentlemen? Why don't the three of you get reacquainted, you can fill him later Daniel."

The Colonel was evidently not used to having very many people speak to him in the commanding tone used by this teenager, and he certainly didn't take orders from civilians. Colonel Hart looked like he was about to say something, but then his face softened as he realized he was this young woman's guest. "Yes ma'am," he said.

Daniel looked at Jaime with a newfound respect. There weren't very many people out there, he thought, Colonel Hart would take orders from, but he looked like he was going to let this one pass.

The four adults made small talk as they ate their breakfast.

"Ms.—I didn't get your name," said the Colonel

"Iron, Jaime Iron," Jaime said as she extended her hand in the direction of the colonel.

The Colonel took her hand graciously and said, "Ms. Iron I am Colonel James Hart, pleased to meet you. I must say, these are the finest biscuits I have eaten since . . ." pain formed on the soldier's face, "well these are the finest biscuits I've eaten since my . . . well since my wife passed on four years ago."

"Well thank you Colonel. Sorry to hear about your wife. She must have been a wonderful woman. She also must have been . . ." Jaime pondered what to say for a moment before finally asking, "what happened to her Colonel?"

"Your sympathy is appreciated Ms. Iron."

"Please call me Jaime," she interrupted.

"Okay Jaime, I'll call you by your given name only if you'll do me the honor of calling me Jim. And yes she was a wonderful woman, much too wonderful to be struck down in the prime of her life."

"What happened," she asked sympathetically.

"She . . ." the colonel paused for a minute as if to collect his thoughts, "she died only a few weeks after being diagnosed with a very rare form of bone cancer." Once again the colonel paused to collect himself. "I sat with her watching her disintegrate before my very eyes. Her bones literally were eaten by her immune system. It was a horrible way to die. All my life, I thought I would be the one to die first. I figured I would be killed in some police action, or some battle fought in a country no one here would have ever heard of. I knew I would be…well you understand, I love this country, almost as much as I loved my wife. I would have done anything to protect my country, my wife, and our way of life. I thought…well I never thought she would die on me."

Jaime looked at the hard stern man wearing camouflage clothes, she saw the pain in his face and for a brief instant there was a hint of moisture in his cold eyes. Then he blinked and the moisture was gone and the steel returned.

"Oh enough," he said as the firmness returned to his voice. "As I was saying you make fine biscuits Jaime."

"And once again thank you Jim, but I didn't really make these biscuits from scratch; I just put them in the oven."

"I know they're not canned biscuits."

"No, they are frozen biscuits they come from a local bakery pre-made. All I have to do is put them in the oven and a few minutes later take them out."

"I see. Well you're a fine cook anyway. Someday when you're grown, you'll make some man a fine wife."

Jaime blushed at the colonel's compliment. "Really Jim, thanks for the compliment, but I believe I am grown. Thirty-nine makes me grown in anyone's eyes doesn't it?"

"No way in hell you're thirty-anything," the colonel said before he remembered what he had seen in the living room.

"You're the girl's mother?" he asked as he motioned to Lavis.

"My Mommy's pretty isn't she?"

"Yes, your mommy is a very pretty lady," the Colonel said with eyes carefully appraising Jaime's fit new body.

They finished their breakfast and the men retired to the living room. Since there was no running water, there wasn't much Jaime could do as far as cleaning the kitchen went. Still she removed the breakfast dishes from the table, wiped them with a paper towel and placed them in the dishwasher. They may not be clean, but at least they were out of sight.

"Who's them two men in there with Daniel?"

"Colonel Hart and Ernie Tabb."

"Are they going to kill Azrael?"

"I don't know. Wherever did you get that idea?"

"I was thinkin' that the old man kinda looks like a big GI Joe."

"He kind of does, doesn't he? You're an awfully observant young lady this morning."

"Mommy what does ov . . . ovserbant mean?"

"Observant, means you pay attention, it means you look at things and see everything there is to see."

"Oh, okay. So are they goin' to kill the angel?"

"I think they're going to try."

"Maybe I'll go in there and tell them how to do it."

"And how would you know?"

"Cause I heard Michael tellin' you how to kill Azrael. He said you had to cut her head off. Maybe I need to tell them how to kill her."

"I've already told them honey, and you don't need to be worrying about killing anything more significant than bugs."

"What's sinificant? Is that like sobverant?"

"No, significant isn't like observant. Significant means important."

"Bugs are important?" Lavis asked with a look of terror in her eyes. "I don't like bugs, 'specially spiders."

"No honey bugs aren't important."

"But you said bugs were sinificant."

"No I said you didn't need to worry about killing anything more important than a bug. It means you don't need to worry about what the men in there are discussing."

"Oh, okay. Mommy when's the power comin' back on? I want to watch Sesame Street."

"I know honey, I want the power to come back on too, but I don't know when. Why don't you stay and help me?"

"Okay, I like helpin' you. You make it fun."

"It's my job, mommies are supposed to make life fun for little girls."

"I don't think that's all mommies are supposed to do," Lavis said seriously, "I think mommies are supposed to do a lot of things. An you make them all fun. I think I'm lucky to have you as a mommy."

"No," Jaime said with tears forming in the corner of her eyes, "I'm the lucky one. I think I'm the lucky one."

Chapter Twenty-Eight

"Okay, what do we know about this angel? How do we kill him? I've got a hard-on for the bastard who killed my men," Colonel Hart said.

"I really don't know much about her…"

"Her? You mean this bastard is female?"

"Yes, I'm not really sure how sexuality works in the Angel world, but Azrael is without a doubt female, and she is extremely powerful…" Daniel was unable to finish before the colonel interrupted, "I saw how powerful this morning when she cut my chopper out of the sky. Finish your report Sergeant."

"Anyway, Azrael is an extremely powerful being; her power is almost unimaginable for me to understand. I…with my own two eyes saw the destruction she was capable of when she wiped out Colbert Heights. As far as I can see she has no weaknesses. If we are able to kill her, we'll have to surprise her somehow."

"So, how do you kill an angel?" Ernie Tabb asked.

"Oh, I didn't tell you, we have to remove her head with the sword. Jaime said Michael told her the only way to kill an angel was decapitation." "I'd rather do it with an armored division," interrupted Colonel Hart. "Yeah, an attack with an armored division would be easier to plan probably, but it isn't possible. I think we have to find out what her weakness is…if she has one."

"So how do we find out her weakness?" asked Ernie.

"I don't really know. We have to plan this somehow in absence of hard information."

Jaime had been listening to the conversation, and felt she could, or should have some input. After all Michael had given her the sword. "Lavis, go to your room. I need to discuss something with these gentlemen."

"But Mommy I…"

"No arguments young lady."

"Yes ma'am."

"Colonel, what kind of information do we need? About Azrael I mean."

"Well we need to know what makes her tick. We need to know what she's afraid of, or rather since she's probably not afraid of anything, what would make her . . . well I need to know how to surprise her."

"I know you can't slip up on her and cut her head off by surprise. I already tried. She's so incredibly fast she…well I couldn't…I tried."

"You tried to what?" asked the Colonel.

`"I already tried to cut her head off. I had my one chance for success before she knew I had the angel's sword, but now she knows I have it. I don't think I, or even one of you can surprise her again. She knows we

212

have the sword and want to kill her. She's going to be impossible to surprise."

"What we need is information. I . . ." the Colonel seemed to ponder for a minute before saying. "Jaime did you say another angel gave you that sword?"

"Yeah, the Archangel Michael. Why?"

"So, there is someone or something out there you have had contact with that knows Ms. Azrael intimately?"

"I guess...but I don't really see what good that's going to do us."

"Information, Jaime, information. To be successful on this or any battlefield, a good commander needs information. The more information he or she has, the better chance he has to plan an operation which will be successful. Every foe, no matter how seemingly invincible the foe seems, has a weakness. We have to find her weakness and exploit it."

"I see what you're saying, but I don't see how we're going to find out what her weakness is."

"Is there any way you can contact the Angel Michael?"

"I don't really know. Maybe I could...if I took the sword I think maybe I can."

"Maybe you could do what?" Daniel asked

"I don't know maybe I could use it to…you know transport myself to where Michael is and…I don't know maybe ask him to tell me about her. There has to be some reason…well there has to be some reason she is killing these girls. Doesn't there? I mean there has to be something in her background, some reason, there has to be something these girls represent to her, something she's missing maybe. Or maybe she thinks something was taken away from her and in turn she is taking or trying to take it away from me in return. I think Michael can tell me what she's missing…tell me what was taken from her. I think we are not dealing with a sane being. I think she is disturbed, and I think there has to be some reason for this. Maybe Michael is the only one who can help us. I hope he can. If he can't tell us; I don't know who or what can."

Colonel Hart sat for a moment and pondered what Jaime had said. After a brief silence, he asked, "Do you think Michael will actually help you kill Azrael?"

"Colonel, I mean James, the answer is no. I don't think that Michael will help me or rather us kill a fellow angel. I do think Michael is sickened by what Azrael is doing. I do think he will give me the information we need. All I can do is ask."

The three of them agreed Jaime would see if the angel Michael could give them any information on Azrael, so Jaime took the sword from Daniel and thought of Michael and in a moment was gone.

It was almost an hour before Jaime returned. When she reappeared, she looked fresher than she had before she disappeared. "I think this will help," she said as she removed what looked like a large folded sheet of paper from one of her pockets.

As Jaime unfolded the paper, it became apparent that this was no ordinary piece of paper. It was one of the 3-d photographs similar to the ones that had been mailed to the parents of the murdered children. When Jaime had finished unfolding the piece of photo, it was about the size of a small color television and contained a moving scene.

"Michael said we were to each take hold of a corner of the photo and we would be transported into the scene. He seemed to think whatever this scene is would be important to our decisions.

As one the four each took a corner of the photo and were immediately transported to a place beyond their experiences.

Chapter Twenty-Nine

The four travelers stood and looked around them in wonder. What was this place? They seemed to be at the edge of a wonderful city, the city gleamed as if it were a polished jewel. This place was amazing. People walked around—at least the travelers thought they were people—seemingly without purpose. It was as if these people had nowhere to go and all day to get there.

"What is this place?" asked Daniel. "Do you think this is heaven?"

"No," Jaime said, "I think this is something else entirely. I think this is …well I think this is Azrael's when."

"What do you mean Azrael's when?" asked Ernie. "Do you think this is…what do you think or rather when do you think this is?"

"I believe this is an ancient city, and these are an ancient people. Look at the sky, there is no sun in the sky, and look at the mist rising from the ground. I think this is a time before the flood of Noah."

"You think they had technology like this," Daniel exclaimed as he looked at the massive machinery which seemed to be moving grain out of what looked like fields of corn in the distance. "I've never heard…well I never thought about there being a technological society before us."

"Why not? Why wouldn't there have been? Remember man lived for hundreds of years before the flood. And these men were but one or two generations removed from God. Look what we have with our limited intelligence created in the past, say three hundred years. Why couldn't these people who were probably significantly more intelligent than we are have created the same or even better things? Remember they lived hundreds of years and Genesis Chapter six verse four says *There were giants in the earth in those days and also after that, when the sons of God came in unto the daughters of men and they bare children to them, the same became mighty men which were of old, men of renown.* I think the bible verse means; not only were they larger than we are today, but like Einstein and Alexander Graham Bell, giants in intelligence also."

"I've never thought about it. I guess I've always believed we were the…wait a minute, if there was a society before us this technologically advanced wouldn't we have found some of their…well I don't know," Daniel looked out at what in his mind was some kind of weird threshing machine wading through a field of wheat, "Wouldn't we have found something like…?" he pointed at the machine.

"Do you think a flood of a magnitude which could destroy the whole earth would not also destroy everything man had created? Genesis Chapter seven verse four says*: For yet seven days, and I will cause it to rain upon the earth forty days and forty nights; and* *every substance that I have made will I blot out from the face of the earth."*

"So you're saying the flood would have wiped this out? You think that it would have destroyed all of this?"

Well Genesis Seven verses nineteen and twenty says: *And the waters prevailed exceedingly upon the earth; and all the high hills, that were under the whole heaven were covered. Fifteen cubits upward did the waters prevail; and the mountains were covered.* I take the verse to mean the highest Mountain was covered by fifteen cubits of water."

"How much is a cubit?" asked Colonel Hart.

"According to most sources it would be from eighteen inches to twenty-two inches, but in reality it is the distance from the elbow to the tip of the middle finger. Now if we're measuring according to these giants, it would probably be more than three feet."

"So you're saying the highest mountain was covered by at least forty-five feet of water?" Daniel asked.

"No, I'm not saying it, the Bible says it," Jaime said. "Now what would you say . . . or rather how far above sea level would you say we are? A hundred feet maybe? And Mt. Everest is what twenty-nine thousand feet? Put twenty-nine thousand and forty five feet of water above us and what do you think would remain. Everything would be crushed, nothing would remain."

A woman of incomparable beauty walked past them, startling the travelers out of their biblical discussion. "Look," said Jaime, "it's Azrael." Azrael didn't have any wings, and wasn't wearing a brown cloak. She walked past them wearing beautiful green samite gown.

"Let's follow her, see where she goes," Jaime said as she ran to keep up with the stride of the giant woman.

They walked through what could have only been a marketplace and watched as Azrael selected fruits and vegetables with unknown names and tastes. All around them people talked, but not in a language any of them could identify.

Azrael strolled through the city, taking her time, not seeming to be in a hurry. She was better dressed than most of the residents of the city, indicating she was maybe a merchant's wife or daughter, or maybe even a noblewoman. People throughout the city showed her deference and smiled as she approached them, stopping to converse with more than a few. She seemed to be genuinely well liked.

As they wound through the city streets, they kept a close eye on Azrael while marveling at the magnificent city. Wealth and beauty was displayed openly, but everywhere they went, no one was more beautiful than Azrael.

Finally after what seemed like hours—but couldn't have been more than thirty minutes—they came to what at first they thought was another of the large markets. As they came closer, they realized it wasn't a market, but a private residence—Azrael's residence?

They followed her inside, and saw her converse with what must have been servants—or maybe slaves—while continually making her way into the inner reaches of what even in this magnificent city was a residence without equal. As they walked through the home, they saw the beautiful 3-d photographs of Azrael, a handsome man, and a little girl who looked like a photocopy of Lavis Ann. Jaime stood for a minute looking at the photograph feeling—knowing—the photographs were somehow important.

Jaime looked at the photograph hanging on the wall for only a second longer, before she hurried to catch up with the woman/angel who had killed her daughter in Jaime's own time. Walking around a corner, Jaime saw Azrael walk out into a garden arranged in a center courtyard. There, she for the first time began to understand why Azrael was killing blonde-blue-eyed children.

A broken child's body lay at the edge of the garden. It was obvious the child had fallen from a great height. As Azrael rushed to the child's body, a figure appeared, and they saw the child's spirit rise from the lifeless body and take an Angel by the hand. Distraught beyond compare, Azrael rushed to the Angel and withdrew the *Angel's Sword* from his belt.

She made one quick swing and the Angel's head toppled to the ground.

Immediately there was a group of angels standing around the fallen angel, as if in amazement one of their own could have been beheaded. Then came the brightest light anyone had ever seen. The light seemed to emanate from everywhere and nowhere at the same time while concealing the form of the being in the light.

A commanding voice spoke in a language everyone understood:

"My daughter Miranda, born of Eve, why have you killed my Angel? I curse you from this day forward. From this day forward you shall be called Azrael— murderer—as you are today, you shall remain until your head is taken in combat. There has never been a fear of death, however because of your transgression you shall become the most feared and hated of all the angels. Be content with what you are for that you shall remain—ALONE—until another makes the same transgression or until the second coming of my son The Christ."

As soon as the last word was formed, the woman was transformed. They saw her begin her transformation, but before it was completed, they were once again standing in the living room of Jaime's house all of them holding on to the corner of a simple sheet of average, white, twenty-pound, Xerox paper.

"What did we just see?" Ernie asked. "Was that what I think it was? Was that how Azrael became the angel of death?"

"I think it was. I think God is punishing her for killing one of his angels. What was it he said?" asked Jaime.

"Such as you are now, you shall remain until your head is taken in combat." Daniel said.

"What exactly does that mean?" asked the Colonel.

"I think she is stuck with a job she didn't want or ask for until someone kills her. Didn't he also say she would be the most hated and feared of the angels? And didn't he say that she would be *alone?*" asked Jaime.

"I think now I know why she's doing what she is doing. And I think I know of a way to stop her," said Colonel James Hart.

The three listened as Colonel Hart outlined a plan.

Chapter Thirty

I don't know if I like this plan," Jaime said trepidation and worry lining her youthful face. "I don't think it will work, and if even one thing goes wrong, it could be disastrous."

Colonel Hart looked at Jaime, knowing, or at least he thought he knew how she felt, and his heart went out to her. He was asking her to make a grave sacrifice. One which may cost her the only daughter she had left. He thought back to when he had lost Mildred, and he felt he knew exactly what she was feeling. If this plan didn't work, she would lose her daughter. Colonel Hart had lost men under his command, but losing soldiers was different. The men he had lost either volunteered or had been drafted into the military. This little girl had done neither.

"Colonel, what do you think our chances of success are?" asked Daniel. Daniel had come to care very much for the little girl, and lately had been having serious thoughts to being exactly what Lavis had asked him only a day or so ago. He was thinking seriously about being her daddy. Lavis was right; a little girl needed a daddy.

"Fifty to seventy-five percent."

Jaime looked at the colonel, a look of abject horror on her face. "You mean you think there is a twenty-five to fifty percent chance I'm going to lose my girl? Not acceptable odds Colonel. We have to think of something else. I won't...I can't lose Lavis. We won't...she won't go along with this. I won't allow it."

"Mommy, I think I can do it," said Lavis Ann.

The four adults turned to look at the little blonde-blue-eyed breath of fresh air. Until now they had thought they were alone. They hadn't realized they were being overheard by a small child.

"No. Honey I don't think I am going to let you do this. I can't bear the thought..."

"Mommy I listened to the whole thing. I think it's our only chance. I can do it, ifin you will let me do it."

"Honey, no."

"Mommy, Azrael is gonna kill me anyway, isn't she. I don' think we can stay here forever without power an water. Do you? I think we have to do somethin' don' you?"

"Yeah. Honey I do think we will have to do something however I don't think this is it. I don't want to lose you too."

"Mommy, you will never lose me. Ifin somethin' happens to me, I'll go be with baby Jesus. God will take care of me. But I'll always be with you. If I can't really be here, I'll be in your thoughts. I'll be in your memories. Somebody has to do somethin' about the angel. I don' think she's supposed to be doing what she's doing, do you?"

"No honey, I don't think she's supposed to be doing what she's doing. But I don't think you need to worry about . . . I don't think you need to be a part of it."

"Mommy I'm already a part of it. She isn't here to kill you, she's here to kill me. We already lost Connie, an I think ifin we don't do something, you'll lose me too."

"Let me think about it," Jaime said with tears once again running down her face. "I...really have to think about it. I don't want to lose you."

"You're a good Mommy. Ever little girl should have a mommy like you. You're always looking out for me."

"That's...that's my job. I'm supposed to look out for you and protect you."

"Then Mommy you have to see keeping me here forever won't protect me. Sooner or later I'm gonna have to go back to school. I've got friends there; an I don't think the teachers will like it ifin I stay in this house forever. I can't stay here forever, can I?"

Jaime looked up at the adults, her face a mask of fear running with deep rivulets of tears. One by one, all of the adults shook their head, confirming they agreed with the little girl. All except Jaime, she didn't agree with Lavis. She didn't agree with any of this. She couldn't bear the thought of being alone again. She had been alone from the time she was ten until she had met Arnold. Arnold had given her a family, and now it was all being taken from her and there wasn't a damn thing she could do about it. But she could do something about it. She, Jaime Iron—formerly Jaime White orphan loved by none—wasn't an orphan anymore. She was loved by many. *I still feel like a lost little girl,* she thought. *For the first time I am somebody, I'm Lavis's Mother. I'm somebody important, at least to this little girl. What will I be if she's gone? Once again I will be an orphan, a woman with no family. I can't ever be crazy and alone again.*

"Jaime," Daniel pulled Jaime into an embrace, holding her tear-stained face against his powerful chest, "it's the only way. I'm sorry baby."

"Don't you sorry me. You don't know what it's like. She's my little girl. Mine. You don't understand you've never had children. I can't have anymore. I've already lost one little girl. I lost my Connie Kay I can't bear to lose Lavis too. It's so damned easy for you to sit there and make decisions in which you have no emotional stake. She's not your daughter, she's mine." Jaime pushed Daniel away and ran down the hallway, slamming the bedroom door behind her.

Three adult men and one small child stood in the hallway.

"What now?" said Colonel Hart.

"We get me ready," said Lavis. I know my mommy is scared. I'm scared too, but she'll see it's the only way."

It was almost an hour before the quartet in the living room heard the door to the bedroom open and saw Jaime come walking back down the hallway. Jaime's face was wet still and her eyes were puffy and blood shot. She must have gushed out water like a wet-weather spring, because not only was her face still wet, her hair was darkened in several places indicating it too was wet.

When Jaime finally spoke, there was still an emotional catch in her voice. "Okay, I'll let her do it, but I will be the one with the sword."

"Jaime no, you can't," Daniel began, but Jaime cut him off. "Yes. Daniel that's the way it is. If I'm going to risk my little girl, I will be the one holding the sword. It was given to me, and I think if Michael had intended for one of you to be the one who kills Azrael, he would have given the weapon to you. I thought this over . . . maybe not entirely rationally but I did think it over and came to the conclusion I may have needed your help in planning this, but I think I will have to be the one swinging the sword."

"No. Jaime, let one of us…" Jaime once again cut Daniel off. "Daniel, this is the only way. If we don't do it my way, we don't do it and the three of you can get out of my house. This is the way it is—period."

The men looked at one another agreeing they disagreed with Jaime Iron, but she didn't seem to give them any other options. It seemed it was going to be her way, or the highway.

"Now, since we've got this settled, we have some preparations to make. I have an old *Singer* sewing machine in the garage. The *Singer* doesn't need power to operate. I think to make this work, I'll have to go shopping and get as close as I can to the outfit she wore. I'm not sure if I can make it, but I think I can make a close replica of it. Gentlemen you get my sewing machine out of the garage and I'll be right back." Jaime picked up the sword, walked into the dining room and picked up her purse off of the dining room table, looked at the three men and her daughter and vanished.

"Well," Ernie Tabb said, "I think that seems to be settled. Let's go see if we can find an old *Singer.*"

It took the three men almost an hour to clear a path wide enough to move the *Singer* inside. Ernie and Daniel carried the ancient machine into the kitchen while Colonel Hart held the kitchen door open. When they had the sewing machine sitting in the middle of the dining room floor, Lavis appeared with a dust cloth and a can of *Pledge* sprayed down the old wood and wiped the dust off of it.

Daniel looked at the old machine, remembering his mother had once sewed on a machine exactly like this one. He could remember her sitting at the machine for hours at a time, her foot rocking back and forth rhythmically on the treadle. The sound had been so comforting and relaxing. Daniel would be playing in the floor, rolling the wooden trucks or setting up his little green army men into platoons as his mother sat there for hours at a time her foot moving up and down, back and forth, sometimes fast sometimes slow, comfortable and relaxed as tranquilly she made or mended the clothes her family wore.

In addition to making clothes for her own family, Daniel's mother had taken in clothes from other families. She mended these clothes mostly for extra money, but sometimes she did this work for free. She made most of her money making dresses for women in upper classes of society. Her work had been without a doubt exquisite, but even though her work was exquisite, even the upper class in Southern Alabama back then had been poor. As a result, even though both of Daniel's parents had worked hard, they had never had much in the way of material things.

Daniel had grown up thinking he would never be poor even if it killed him. As he grew older, he never realized even though he could no longer be considered poor, he lived a life that up until now had been poor in spirit. He wasn't or would never be monetarily poor, but he had been living a very spare existence without love. Only now did he realize Jaime was far richer in terms of family than was he.

Daniel had been so steadfast in his quest to become affluent, he had forgotten life was more than money. They had been poor when he grew up, but they'd had a loving home. Love was something Daniel could honestly say he hadn't missed until the last few days. Seeing Jaime interact with her daughter these last few days had really made Daniel miss having a family. He had spent more than forty years building a great wealth, and now realized he had no family, no heirs.

He didn't know if he would get to keep this new body when all of this was over, but even if he didn't he now knew, given a chance he would be this little girl's father. He would accept the responsibility, gladly, without reservation. He already was beginning to love the impetuous little girl. She may be full of questions, but she was asking questions for a reason. She really wanted to know the answers. Even now she had a brace of questions being directed at the colonel. Daniel looked at the girl for the first time through eyes which found the questions not maddening, through ears that heard the inquisition as the sincere effort of a young girl trying her best to understand the world around her. She asked the questions endeavoring to comprehend maddening events that made even the eldest among them scratching his head in wonder. He would have never believed he would ever be thinking of becoming someone's father, not to mention the added benefits associated with being the girl's father—namely being the husband to Jaime Iron.

But for all of it to take place they had to first kill an angel. Before he could become a husband and father, he had—they had to first kill a being who wasn't mortal, a being far more powerful than any weapon created by man. There was only one way to kill the angel, according to Jaime, who had been instructed by Michael, the only way to kill Azrael was to cut her head off with the sword furnished by Michael. He hoped the plan would work—it had to work, if it didn't they would probably all lose their lives. Being killed today didn't seem as important as it had only days ago. Days ago he hadn't believed in immortal lives, the immortal soul, heaven, or hell. Today, he believed. He had been down on his knees and prayed the prayer of a sinner, he had acknowledged he was imperfect and asked for forgiveness of his sins. He hoped it would be enough, if it wasn't though, he would carry it to his grave in ignorance, for he had done everything he could for now.

Jaime reappeared holding two bags filled with sewing supplies and four bolts of luxurious cloth. "This is the closest thing I could find. I hope it will be close enough," she said looking uncertain. "I'm not sure I can make the outfit we saw but I will try." She lay the bolts of cloth to the side of the sewing machine, walked down the hall and into a room on the right side of the hall. Jaime was absent from their sight for a short time before she returned with a large—looked like a tackle box—box and three pairs of scissors(one huge pair, the blades of which were at least a foot long, a medium sized pair, and a tiny pair, Daniel knew were for removing bad stitches).

Jaime walked back into the dining room, pulled one of the chairs from the dining room table and sat down at the sewing machine and started to work on the most important article of clothing she had ever designed.

Everything was ready—as ready as four adults and one mortal child could make it—for the planned murder of God's Angel of Death. They'd gone over the plan again and again. Everything had been planned and orchestrated as closely as they could. Only no one really knew if it would work. They could only hope.

It had taken Jaime more than ten hours of constant measuring and sewing to get the outfit right. The three men sat and watched her trying not to say anything—her tears flowed constantly the entire time—they could tell this weighed heavy on her heart. She was doing something against her will; something she believed would get her daughter killed. If this didn't work, it had all been for nothing.

Chapter Thirty-One

They decided even if Azrael reappeared now, they would wait until morning before they did anything. Their plan didn't necessarily depend on what the actual time was, as much as it did that they were all well rested. It was now nearly ten at night. Lavis had been in the bed for more than two hours, but the adults weren't really sleepy.

Jaime knew she couldn't sleep if she tried. She kept going back in her thoughts to Azrael's time—what they had seen—had Azrael actually been mortal at one time? Still, Jaime couldn't imagine anything driving her into doing what the Angel of Death was now doing. This was crazy. How could she justify herself to anyone? How could God let one of his Archangels terrify a whole town? Was this part of some kind of cosmic plan mere mortals couldn't possibly understand?

There were those and a hundred other questions as Jaime and the other three adults sat in the living room in the twilight produced by the coal-oil lantern. A few minutes to eleven, Daniel got up, took her by the hand and said, "let's go to bed hon. Colonel, you and Ernie will find two other bedrooms. The beds are made, you may go to bed whenever you like."

"We will Daniel. I think it will be soon."

By midnight, the house was silent, the only noise coming from the soldiers standing at the perimeter of the Circle. Inside the house was dark and silent, outside, soldiers milled around trying to understand exactly what was going on, and why they were there.

Morning came before anyone wanted it to. The Sun rose, and an azure blue sky appeared. With the rising sun, came Azrael in all her glory. She appeared outside the protected property line, visible to everyone, soldiers included.

Azrael began to sing, exactly as she had the morning before.

SHALL WE GATHER AT THE RIVER

CONNIE KAY IS DOWN AT THE RIVER

SHE'S GATHERED WITH THE DEAD AT THE RIVER

THAT FLOWS WITH THE BLOOD OF THE SLAIN

YES WE'LL GATHER AT THE RIVER

THE BEAUTIFUL YET HORRIBLE RIVER

GATHER WITH CONNIE KAY AT THE RIVER

AND DROWN HER IN THE BLOOD OF THE SLAIN

SOON LAVIS ANN WILL REACH THE RIVER

THAT AWFUL AND BLOOD DARK RIVER

SOON LAVIS AND CONNIE WILL BE TOGETHER

FOREVER WITH THE REST OF THE SLAIN

YES LAVIS ANN WILL SEE THE RIVER

THAT BEAUTIFUL BLOOD DARK RIVER

SHE'LL GATHER WITH THE DEAD AT THE RIVER

AND I'LL DROWN HER IN THE BLOOD OF THE SLAIN

Jaime along with the rest of the world close enough to hear Azrael belting out her bastard version of the hymn awoke. She wanted to scream at Azrael, wanted to…well the things she wanted to do, a nice lady didn't discuss. But if everything worked out as they had planned and hoped they would, they would be rid of Azrael for good today.

"Is it time Mommy?" asked Lavis who was suddenly at the foot of the bed in which Daniel and Jaime lay.

"What? Time for what?" asked Jaime surprised by her daughter's appearance.

"You know time for what we planned yesterday. I noticed my outfit was ready, so I already put it on. How does it look?"

Jaime looked at her daughter, hoping once again this plan would work. "It looks wonderful, you look wonderful baby."

"I'm not a baby anymore. Wish you would quit callin' me that"

"I know you're not a baby anymore, I…well you will always be my baby."

"I know." Lavis said with conviction. "So are we ready?"

"Give us a chance to get up and get around first. Don't be in such a hurry young lady. Go on in the living room and give us a chance to get up and get dressed."

"Okay," said Lavis as she turned and raced down the hall in the outfit Jaime spent so much time on yesterday.

Jaime turned to Daniel and kissed him on the cheek. "Do you think this will work," she asked.

"I don't know. I hope so. I think it's our only chance though, don't you?"

"I don't know. I wish there were some other way though. I wish I didn't have to put Lavis at risk. She's just a baby regardless what she thinks."

"I know."

Jaime and Michael Bordeaux walked into the living room to find Colonel Hart and Ernie Tabb sitting on the couch with Lavis Ann between them. Outside Azrael still sung her hymn at an impossible volume, louder than even yesterday morning. Jaime figured the soldier's—if they weren't wearing earplugs—ears were bleeding.

"Is everyone ready, does everyone know their job," Colonel Hart asked.

"I know my job," Lavis said proudly. "I'm supposed to run across the yard and out into the circle of mud. When I see Azrael I'm supposed to run to her calling her Mommy. I'm supposed to run to her like she was my mommy. That's right isn't it?"

"Yes. Honey it's what you're supposed to do. You be careful honey I don't think I could bear to lose you."

"I will Mommy."

"Colonel Hart asked, "Daniel are you clear on what you're supposed to do?"

"Yeah, I'm supposed to let her get halfway across the yard then come out of the house and yell at her to stop, not to cross the…well whatever it is…out of the safe zone for lack of a better word. I'm supposed to yell at her not to leave the yard."

Well this Azrael doesn't know either me or Ernie is here so we're going to stay out of sight. This is your game kids, it's time to play. Jaime you stand inside the door and hold the sword. When Lavis reaches the girl, regardless what happens, you flash in behind her and remove her head. This will be over then supposedly. Right?"

"We can only hope," answered Jaime.

"Let's do it then."

"Anytime you're ready Lavis," Colonel Hart said.

Chapter Thirty-Two

Lavis walked out onto the porch, feigning rubbing the sleep out of her eyes. She turned around and looked at the door which she had come out. Then she began her walk across the yard. Lavis didn't seem hurried at first; then she suddenly seemed to see the angel. "Mommy," she cried as she ran in the direction of the angel.

Daniel could see the angel smile—she kind of looked like the fox you have given keys to the henhouse—in recognition. Then the smile faded, replaced by a look of uncertainty as Lavis got closer. He was running after Lavis calling her name, but the angel was doing something different. She was doing something they had hoped for, but hadn't really expected. Azrael had dropped her angel's sword and was on her knee, her arms outstretched calling a name—at least it sounded like a name—in a language un-spoken in more years than were numbered or remembered.

Jaime watched in horror as her daughter ran to the angel of death. *This has got to work,* she thought. When Azrael stretched out her arms as if in recognition of the young girl, Jaime knew she had her. Jaime held her breath and waited against all her better judgment until the Colonel removed his hand from her arm. With one thought she flashed across the distance, appearing directly behind Azrael exactly as Lavis rushed into her arms.

Without even a second thought, Jaime swung the sword in a wide arc, knowing the angel's back was turned, knowing her attention was on the young girl, knowing soon she would be a murderer. Knowing one of God's most beautiful, powerful beings had to die.

No. This isn't murder, this is self-defense. This is protecting my child. I am doing exactly what the police do. I am protecting and defending my little girl, she thought. The sword whistled through the air, Jaime's Mind's Eye seeing the angel's head removed from her shoulders.

The ***Mind's Eye*** can be deceptive.

Jaime watched as the angel disappeared. Jaime's sword instead of removing the angel's head, came down squarely in the center of Lavis's forehead, splitting her head open like a ripe melon and cleaving her all the way down to her shoulders. Lavis dropped like a stone.

Jaime dropped to her knees, the sword forgotten, everything forgotten except her precious baby.

As the girl's spirit rose out of the shell she had once inhabited, the killer wiped a tear from what had only a moment ago been a dry eye and instructed the little girl's soul on the way to the Heavenly Father, watching as one of the lesser angels came to show the young girl the way. "Good bye sweet Lavis Ann," said the killer, "Good bye," muttered Jaime.

Jaime turned to see Daniel Bordeaux running across the yard, pistol drawn, chased by another agent, the man who had been with him the first day he appeared at her door. Jaime seemed to remember his name being Ben something or other. But the Daniel walking toward her wasn't Daniel from a few minutes ago. He was older and fat and tired...Daniel Bordeaux didn't look anything like *her Daniel*. Jaime looked down at her body, and was not surprised to see she had returned to her normal thirty-nine year old body. Did she really expect to be able to keep that nineteen year old body forever? Well it was obvious she wouldn't/couldn't.

Jaime looked up into his eyes, expecting to see compassion, love, anything except what she saw. Jaime saw a face that held not compassion and empathy, but a grim face full of resignation, disgust and maybe a little relief.

"Daniel. I'm sorry," she began as she started to cry.

Daniel never said a word. He reached down and deftly and quickly manacled her with a set of handcuffs.

"What...what are you doing?"

"You have the right to remain silent."

Jaime really didn't hear the words as she looked around in wonder. No longer was there a strip of mud surrounding her home. Everyone's home had reappeared. People were standing in their yards looking at the big cop leading their neighbor to a car parked in her driveway.

"You have the right to be represented by legal counsel. If you cannot afford counsel…"

What in hell was going on? "Daniel what are you…why are you arresting me?"

"Miranda White do you understand these rights?"

Miranda White, who was Miranda White, wondered Jaime.

Daniel led her to the car, as Jaime stared at her surroundings with wonder. How had everything come back? Jaime looked at her home, and was surprised to see it wasn't her home. Instead of the beautiful half-brick home she was accustomed to seeing, someone or something had replaced it with an ancient looking frame home. It looked to be about the same size as her home, and it faced the proper way, but it wasn't her home. Her home was a beautiful home, with a perfectly landscaped yard. The yard here didn't look like it had been mowed in weeks. The only thing which looked exactly like she remembered it was the magnificent Oak standing in the front yard. It looked the same as always.

Daniel opened the back door to a Chevrolet Tahoe, and placed his hand on the top of Jaime's head. "I don't want you to hit your head as you get in Ms. White."

"Why do you keep calling me Ms. White? My name is Jaime. Jaime Iron. Daniel don't you remember?"

"Ms. White, your name is Miranda White, and I've been looking for you a long time, almost six years."

"Daniel, what are you talking about?"

"Ms. White, my name isn't Daniel. I am Detective Michael Bordeaux. Ms. White, I don't know what kind of game you're...you have been playing, but it's over. Understand?"

The Truth

Chapter Thirty-Three

About one week later

Michael Bordeaux stood in a small room looking at Miranda White through a one-way glass. She seemed to be content, and didn't seem to be any danger to herself or anyone else. She seemed calm and her thoughts seemed to be collected. No one would ever know by looking at her the proclivity for violence she possessed. If you met her on the street, she would seem normal enough; but knowing what he knew about Miranda he would never turn his back on her.

Michael turned to the door as a slightly built older black man about Michael's age walked in. Michael greeted the Doctor and asked, "So Dr. Tabb what's the consensus?"

"The consensus on what?"

"What's her mental state, can she stand trial?"

"In my opinion, no. She has suffered a severe break with reality. Ms. Miranda White has…"

"I know you could render me speechless with a bunch of words and phrases I don't understand Doctor. But could you possibly dumb it down enough for an ancient state cop?"

"In layman's terms?"

"Yeah, layman's terms."

"She's nuts. She is a paranoid schizophrenic and she also has multiple personalities or Dissociative Identity Disorder. Ms. White's disorder is unique, her personalities interact with each other. She has more than twenty distinctive personalities we've identified so far."

"I figured as much."

"Mr. Bordeaux, tell me what has happened to Miranda since she left us."

"I'm Michael or Detective...I answer to Detective more than anything else. This is what we know. Miranda White was born July 12th thirty-nine years ago. Her mother died in childbirth, and she was raised by her dad. Apparently—now this is according to court documents—about the age of ten, her dad decided it was time for young Miranda to take her mother's place in his bed and he began molesting her. This incest continued until his death of lung cancer when she was twelve.

When he died, she became an orphan. Now you've been a doctor long enough to know no-one adopts twelve year olds. Adopting families want babies. Miranda became a ward of the state and was bounced from foster home to foster home until she was fourteen.

When she was fourteen, she moved in with a new foster family. The Dodge family. Soon Miranda accused Mr. Dodge of sexually assaulting her. It's not clear whether the alleged assault happened or if it was a complete fabrication. Rape allegations by foster children back then weren't always investigated thoroughly. Miranda was placed with another family, two days after the placement she ran away, caught a ride back to the Dodge home and killed David Dodge and his family with a machete she picked up in the family garage. She never admitted to anything.

The ferocity of the crime demanded she be tried as an adult, but she was found incompetent to stand trial, as a result she came here to Taylor Hardin Secure Medical Facility. Miranda spent three years here, without a single incident noted in her file. She followed orders and didn't rock the boat so to speak. Since the staff never had any problems with her security around her became lax and eventually they moved her into a minimum security room at Bryce Hospital. She shared a room with a girl about her age named Jaime Iron."

"I know about all her history here Detective, I want to know what she's been doing since she left us twenty-years ago."

Two months after her eighteenth birthday, Miranda picked up a staff member's jacket and badge, walked right out the front door of Bryce Hospital and completely disappeared. She took

Jaime Iron's identity and somehow got into college, graduated, got a job with a bank. How she passed the background check we don't really know.

Miranda left the bank after only fourteen months, and is remembered as an excellent employee. She went to work for a real estate agency in Mobile, Alabama, within two years she was the number one agent. In her ten years working for the agency she earned commissions of more than two million dollars. While she was working for the agency we think she may have been raped. It's speculation, because it was about that time she started killing people…anyway she became pregnant at twenty six, but no one knew who the father was…anytime anyone asked Miranda would tell them her baby's daddy was a banker named Arnold. All sources say Miranda—known to them as Jaime—was an excellent mother.

But excellent mother or not, Miranda's daughter died in a fall from the second story window of their condo. We believe this was nothing more than an accident. According to her boss, after her daughter's death, she tried to work for another few months even after he insisted that she take some time to grieve. Then one day she disappeared.

About that time, Miranda came onto our radar. She had been living in Mobile for fourteen years; but her daughter's death changed everything. She must've snapped because six girls in the Mobile/Prichard area went missing in the six months following her daughter's death. She left fingerprints all over the crime scenes and we quickly identified Miranda White. We've been chasing her for the past six years, and we had no idea what she looked like. The last photograph of Miranda White was taken when she was fourteen years old the day she arrived at Taylor. When we started looking for Miranda she was thirty-three. We did the age progression from fourteen to thirty-three, but the result wasn't even close. We were not looking for six feet, blonde and blue, we were looking for a five and a half foot brunette. We knew Miranda was somewhere in Northwest Alabama, but Alabama is a large state with a lot of forty year old women. She was kidnapping little girls who looked like her daughter Lavis Ann at the same age. Evidently Miranda sent herself a photograph showing her with two of the girls she had killed. She called and we rushed out to her home thinking we were going to find a young housewife, scared to death. What we found was a crazy woman chasing a young girl across the yard with a sword. She killed a little girl before my eyes Doc."

"I probably don't really want to know the answer to this question, but I've got to ask. How many people has she killed?"

"If you include the Dodge family when she was fourteen, we've identified more than two hundred; but how many is questionable. There are a lot of unsolved murders and closed cases where police departments could have identified the murder victims as a murder-suicide when in reality it could have been Miranda."

"So…she's sacrificed more little girls than just the ones in Alabama?"

"No…no, we kept as much as we could secret. She was only sacrificing little girls in Alabama…the others, she just killed. Sometimes with a knife, some of the victims were strangled, some beaten, never were they killed with a gun. They were all personal hands-on killings. Old men, young men, quadriplegics, healthy young women…no discernible pattern other than messy up close and personal murder."

"All of this in Alabama? How is that possible?"

"No. Remember when I said she earned more than two million dollars in commissions? She invested most of that. Miranda, rather Jaime Irons real estate holdings pay her more than four million dollars a year. She could afford to travel anywhere and do anything. She's roamed all over the United States."

"I see. I wouldn't have considered her quite that dangerous."

"Never underestimate her Doc; she is lethal."

"There is something you will probably want to see."

"What's that?"

"Miranda—we gave her access to a computer with a word processing program and asked her to tell what happened to the child she killed. I think you would be intrigued to read it. It's more than one-hundred pages. She believes the angel of death, an angel named Azrael was trying to kill her two daughters Lavis Ann and Connie Kay. You should read this, you're in it?"

"I'm in it?"

"Yes Detective Bordeaux, you are her love interest. She calls you Daniel in the…I'll call it a book."

"You know she called me Daniel when I arrested her."

"She did?"

"Yeah."

"She's inventive for sure, you started out old, and ended up looking like you were twenty-five. Oh and you were a millionaire."

"My late wife would have been interested to hear it, Doc I raised six girls on a cop's salary. One thing we'll never be is rich."

"I understand that. A state psychiatrist doesn't make much more than a state detective I'm sure."

"So you think she's crazy?"

"She's a loon Agent Bordeaux. Off her rocker. Elevator doesn't go all the way to the top. She's not carrying a full load of bricks. Every phrase you have ever heard describing a crazy person describes this patient."

"So she'll never stand trial?"

"Not in this lifetime. I've got a copy of the book she wrote you get a chance…read it. It's interesting, it would make an interesting movie. Miranda plays every part in the book. She has written it like a screen play, you know what everyone is thinking, you see it from every angle, even when she is supposedly not anywhere around."

"I'll get you my email address, send me a copy for evidence, just in case she ever stands trial."

"She has imagination anyway…If it was true, it would explain the situation very well."

Jaime Iron sat in a room looking at a mirror. She couldn't exactly figure out why she was back in the orphanage where she grew up, but it didn't matter. Jaime could see herself; it was wonderful to be nineteen again. She turned to Azrael who was standing beside her wings spread, an archangel in her full glory. The *Council of Angels* had taken Jaime's sword when Daniel arrested her, so she couldn't kill Azrael. The archangel seemed to find this outrageously funny for Azrael was laughing at her. Azrael laughed so hard, Jaime could feel the ground beginning to shake.

As Azrael, God's supreme angel of death began to sing one of Jaime's favorite hymns. *Shall We Gather At the River.* Jaime began to plan her departure from these accommodations. They just didn't seem to fit her southern belle mentality. The people here treated her as if she were dangerous or something.

Here is the place where I thank everyone who was involved. They are too many to name.

First and foremost I would like to thank my Mother, Tamara(Tam) Barker. More than anyone she instilled a deep love for the written word and always encouraged my imagination. I truly wish she was still here so I could bounce ideas off her.

I would like to thank my Sister, Judy Barker Austin. She helped me with this book, and Co-Authored my first book, **The God Complex: Family Secrets.** She is a blessing to everyone who knows her.

Next in line for the thanks is Charles "Chunky" White. Without his encouragement none of this would have transpired. I wrote the first chapter of The God Complex almost fifteen years ago, and brought it down to him typed out on copy paper. He read it, and looked up at me—I'm 6'9—and asked, "did you write this?" When I answered, "yes." He asked me, "What are you doing driving a truck?"

Through the years, there have been many who offered encouragement, Diane Boyd, Mike Bowman, Connie Bolton, and Dover Edwards. Without them this wouldn't be in print, it would still be molding in the bottom of a closet.

Thank you, each and every one of you.

I truly hope you enjoyed this.

There are mistakes in this book if you are comparing it to the world today. I'm sure the Army and Marines don't function in the way I've painted them, and the information I have on police work came from my dad, Buford Barker. He retired more than three decades ago so I may be a little out of date.

Some of the places in this book are real and the geography and seasons are as described. If you're ever in the area, on a summer day, William's Hollow on Little Bear Creek near Belgreen Alabama is a fantastic little out of the way place to take a dip in the lake. Fife's is a real restaurant in Birmingham, they make a fantastic breakfast, and the Blue Monkey Lounge in Birmingham is a nice place to have a beer or an Alabama Slammer.

THE GOD COMPLEX

FAMILY SECRETS

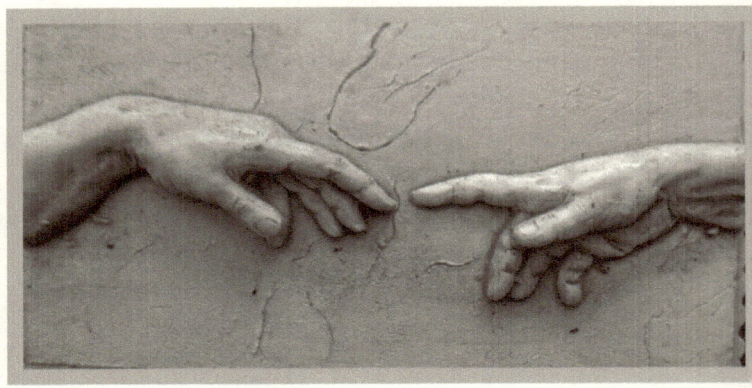

A NOVEL
BY
ROS BARKER
AND
JUDY BARKER AUSTIN

PART ONE –

RUSSELLVILLE, ALABAMA
JUNE 2000

Chapter One

Peter sat at his grandfather's bedside mesmerized by the fragile, brittle shell that poorly represented the strong, physically fit man who had raised him. Even physically spent, Papa still exuded a royal elegance coupled with a commanding spirit that permeated the antique-filled bedroom.

"We hid so much from you about us . . . about you . . . about our true wealth," whispered Papa as a lock of white hair fell down and nestled between his intelligent, piercing eyes. At ninety-five, Papa still sported a full head of white, not gray, hair. He wore it longer than other male senior citizens in the area despite his barber's constant prodding to wear a shorter and more mature style. Peter, had hair as dark as Papa's was white worn in what could be called a military cut.

Peter held back tears as he wondered if his grandfather would live to see another sunrise. Dawn was his Papa's favorite time of day. As far back as Peter could remember, Papa faithfully rose early enough to witness each new day's sunrise.

Because Papa was now bedridden, Peter had hung a gorgeous sunrise portrait of Loch Ness Scotland on the wall across from where Papa lay propped up by a bevy of assorted pillows on a massive, ornately carved canopy bed. Each morning Peter stopped by to check on his grandfather, and they enjoyed discussing the majesty and beauty of the sunrise in the portrait. Peter selected this particular Scottish portrait because Papa was an immigrant from Scotland and believed it might remind Papa of happy times in his homeland.

Papa was a popular and respected man in Franklin County. Local and state officials had pleaded with him since the `50s to run for public office, but he had never so much as run for city council or even deacon in his church.

"Maybe Anna and I should have told you, but we kept it all from you."

Peter couldn't help but smile as his grandfather referred to Gramma Joanna by the shortened version of her name. He hadn't had much to smile about since a frantic Jim Davis, Russellville's Chief of Police, had called back in March.

"I need your help," begged Chief Davis. "I know you're not going to believe this, but Papa's been in another accident. He ran two cars and a chicken truck off the road before he finally ended up in a ditch on Highway 24 across from the Parade Gas Station. He's hurt and refuses to let Clyde, the ambulance driver, take him to the hospital. When Clyde gets too close, Papa pelts him with rocks from the ditch. Papa must have a good throwing arm because Clyde already has a split lip and a swollen eye. Can you get out here and talk some sense into him?"

"Sure, Jim," mumbled Peter. "I'll be right there."

It was the third time in two weeks Papa and his 1979 Cadillac Fleetwood had caused an accident. Chief Davis warned Papa one more would result in his driver's license being revoked and explained this to him at the last accident scene. Papa had stomped the accelerator instead of the brakes at a downtown red light broadsiding a van transporting elderly contestants to the senior citizen center for their annual and highly anticipated *Most Unusual Hat* day. No one was injured, but it was quite a sight to see so many disheveled, pissed-off old folks lined up along Jackson Avenue with their prized, unusual hats all ruined. Papa's Cadillac wasn't even dented by the accident while the van required extensive bodywork.

Peter had left his office and driven as fast as he could to the scene of the accident. Before he opened the door of his Dodge Ramcharger, he heard Papa rant and rave as he threatened to have the Chief fired. When a rock zoomed by his head, Peter called out for Papa to behave. No matter how much Peter reasoned with Papa, he could not talk him into going to the hospital. Papa wanted to go home.

"A hospital is for sick people. I'm not sick," Papa had argued. "If you go into a hospital and you're not sick, you will be by the time you come out, if you come out at all. Doctors bury their mistakes."

Papa hated hospitals to the point where Peter believed Papa actually had a phobia. As far as Peter knew, Papa had never been in a hospital. Peter finally gave in to Papa, paid Clyde extra to transport Papa home, and hired a private medical team to care for Papa until he got his strength back.

Despite superb medical treatment for three months, Papa had not recovered his strength. He had given up, almost willing himself to die. He had lost sixty pounds and could barely speak above a whisper.

"You listen to me, young prince," commanded Papa as he struggled to regain his grandson's attention.

Papa and Gramma Joanna had always called Peter *Prince*, or *young prince*. Peter didn't like it, but at least they only used those endearments in private. Even though Peter was twenty-eight, he still cringed at the thought of anyone finding out about his nickname. *Prince*, thought Peter, *was a dog's name.*

"When Harold presents my new will, you will be displeased," whispered Papa losing the physical strength he had accumulated a few minutes earlier. "I did not leave you everything, but I have provided very well for you."

Papa prayed for sufficient strength to continue as he remembered when Peter was thirteen and Anna passed away. As she died, he promised to reveal their family secrets to young Peter. It was the only promise to her he'd never kept. Numerous times, he'd attempted to tell Peter about their secrets, but each time he'd been afraid of the effect it would have on the young prince.

"Papa, please. You don't have to explain anything," pleaded Peter. "You know I don't and never have cared about money."

"You must listen, Peter. I have not always been so good."

Peter knew how ethical Papa was in both personal and private life. Peter often felt the tremendous weight on his shoulders as he strived to live up to the principles his Papa had taught him. "Papa . . . That's not true. You . . ."

"You don't understand," Papa interrupted. "But I have tried to make amends. That is why I left so much to our employees. There is more . . . so . . . much . . . more . . ."

Papa again labored with what he knew he must tell Peter. His grandson was a good man, not perfect by any means, but a kind man. There were times he and Anna reluctantly reined the boy in, but those rebellious incidents had been few and far between. Besides--Alan usually caused them. Peter, Eric, and Alan, had been inseparable growing up. Eric and Alan had spent about as much time at the Stacia house as Peter had. Even with bad influences, Papa felt Peter had grown into a man of noble character.

"Papa, don't try so hard. You need to . . ."

"You will have great power." Papa interrupted. "Use this power for good, not evil. God will guide you . . . I have set you free . . . Young prince in the back of my Bible in an envelope are three keys . . . I meant to tell you, to protect you, and now . . . I fear . . . I fear it's too late." Papa's voice had continued to grow weaker and softer with his last whispered words. Papa shut his eyes, relaxed his face, and started to breathe in short shallow breaths. Several times Peter thought Papa stopped breathing, but each time was relieved to see his grandfather's chest raise and lower again. Peter didn't know how long he sat there, afraid to move before Papa spoke again. This time, though, Papa did not open his eyes.

"Young prince?"

"Yes, Papa?"

"Will you read me the prayer in my Bible? You know the one. Anna's Prayer?"

"Yes, Papa. I'll read it."

Peter gently opened the tattered Holy Bible on the nightstand and immediately saw the prayer. Every morning his grandmother took the prayer from her Bible, sat in her chair in the living room, and prayed as tears streamed down her face. Peter never understood why this particular prayer affected his Gramma Joanna in the way it did. As he looked at the prayer, he saw many words smeared beyond recognition where his grandmother's tears had fallen on the parchment. It was inconsequential that many of the words were unreadable, because she had known the poem by heart, as did Papa, and as did Peter.

Papa smiled as Peter recited . . .

Give patience, Lord to us Thy children
In these dark, stormy days to bear
The persecution of our people
The tortures falling to our share.

Give strength, just God, to us who need it
The persecutors to forgive
Our heavy, painful cross to carry
And Thy great meekness to achieve.

When we are plundered and insulted
In days of mutinous unrest
We turn for help to Thee, Christ-Savior,
That we may stand the bitter test.

Lord of the world, God of Creation,
Give us Thy blessing through our prayer
Give peace of heart to us, O Master,
This hour of utmost dread to bear.

And on the threshold of the grave
Breathe power divine into our clay
That we, Thy children, may find strength
In meekness for our foes to pray.

As Peter picked up Papa's Bible to return the prayer, an envelope fell to the floor He retrieved it, tore it open, and found three unusual keys inside. As he turned the keys over and over in his hands, questions filled his head. *What are these keys for? Why hadn't Papa given them to me before now? What did Papa mean when he said there were family secrets?*

266

For the first time in his life, he felt weak and helpless.
He realized he was not ready to relinquish Papa's
guidance, wisdom, and love.

He mulled all these things over in his mind oblivious
that during the reading of the poem his beloved Papa,
and greatest man he'd ever known, had reached that
clearing at the end of his path.

In a room nearby, Papa's private duty nurse and
housekeeper heard a bloodcurdling wail and ran into the
bedroom to find Peter sobbing and tightly holding
Papa's frail body.

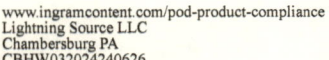